HIS TEMPTATION

X ENTERPRISES BOOK FOUR

TANYA GALLAGHER

PENCHANT PRESS

ISBN: 0-9998620-8-1

ISBN-13: 978-0-9998620-8-7

Cover design by Resplendent Media

Visit: www.tanyagallagherbooks.com

For Jules.

CHAPTER 1

"*T*hree tingling toys to try tonight." Avery Beeker tapped her pen to her lips and squinted at her brainstorming notebook. "Hmm. Should I use *tantalizing* instead of *tingling*?"

Her best friend Sophie Carter pressed the pause button on her DVD player's remote control. "Your adherence to alliteration is admirable."

"And?"

"*And.*" Sophie rolled her eyes. "I see what you're doing there. But use tantalizing. Technically a good vibrator doesn't tingle—it makes *you* tingle."

Avery grinned and circled *tantalizing* in purple ink. "An important distinction. One the X Enterprises audience will be sure to pick up on."

Sophie snorted. "Unlikely. All they want to know, Miss PR, is if the toys can get them off. But that's not the point." She gestured at the notebook propped on Avery's pajama-clad knees. "It's time to put that notebook away." She jerked her head at the *Thor: Ragnarok* credits frozen on her TV screen. "Our pizza should be here any minute, and Chris Hemsworth and Tom Hiddleston wait for no one."

Avery capped her pen and frowned. "I'm just trying to get ahead of the game for Monday."

"Yes, but no one's grading you on your homework," Sophie said. "In

1

fact, I'll bet your boss doesn't care how much time you're putting into things as long as the work gets done."

Avery huffed a sigh and dropped the notebook onto Sophie's coffee table. "Fair point." She twisted her hands together. "It's just that I'm trying to do this right."

"You don't need to compensate for the fact that you're—"

Sophie broke off, and Avery filled in the rest. "A virgin?"

Sophie gave her a sympathetic squeeze on her knee. "It's fine. No one's judging."

Avery groaned. "That's because no one knows. Can you imagine what would happen if my boss found out that the person he hired to write scandalous blog posts and promotional materials has zero first-hand experience having sex with another person? It would end my career before it even got off the ground."

"As long as you're doing your job, it doesn't matter."

Avery gestured at her abandoned notebook. "Which is why I have to kick ass on each and every assignment I complete. I have to be that much more awesome."

"It's still homework." Sophie used one socked foot to nudge the notebook to the far end of the table.

"I don't know if I'd call you a homework expert." Avery smiled so Sophie would know she was joking.

Her friend pressed a hand to her forehead with a dramatic, mock-wounded tone. "You say it like I didn't go to college."

"Oh, Soph. Being enrolled and actually attending class are two different things."

Sophie grinned. "Once again, an important distinction. But let's not forget that I still walked out of college with a job."

Avery tilted her head in acknowledgment. "I have to give you that." For every skipped class, Sophie had been busy growing an online following for her food blog, *Who's Hungry*. She'd started *Who's Hungry* sophomore year, sharing recipes that fellow college students could make in their dorms with limited cooking tools. By senior year she had enough sponsors and social media followers to pull down the same salary she would have made in a full-time job. Soph knew how to hustle—she'd just never had a boss to answer to. Unlike Avery.

Avery propped her feet on the edge of the coffee table and leaned back against Sophie's couch cushions. "How much longer until we can wash off this face mask?" In honor of girls' night in, they'd mixed up some Amazonian clay masks—the kind with apple cider vinegar that made your face smell and that turned everything a sickly gray-green color. It was the best for pulling gunk out of your pores, but god did it reek. Post-pizza, they'd paint their nails while finishing *Thor: Ragnarok*.

"Should be just about when the pizza gets here."

The doorbell rang on cue.

"Can you get that, Ave?" Sophie ducked into the next room, calling over her shoulder, "It's prepaid, so you can just add a tip to the receipt."

Avery unfolded herself from the couch and wove her way to the door. "Yeah, yeah. Ladies and gentlemen, this is the dark side of Insta-fame. Sophie Carter, renowned food blogger extraordinaire, must hide in shame from the pizza delivery man so as not to expose the fact that she's a real human who sometimes wants cheesy, carb-filled splurge food that's—gasp —not homemade."

Sophie laughed. "Or I just don't want him to be scared the next time he sees me since it's kind of a regular thing these days."

"Which is it—hiding a lie or impressing the pizza man? The world may never know." Avery swung open the door on the last line and choked out her next words. "Holy shit."

Geoffrey Carter, Sophie's older brother and the exclusive object of Avery's teen fantasies, stood in the doorway holding a pizza box and wearing a dark, dangerous grin.

Avery's mouth fell open, and she stumbled backward into the apartment. The smell of cheese and sauce wafted through the hallway of Sophie's home, snapping Avery into action.

She reached for the box. "Let me just grab you. *It!* I'll grab *it!*"

Shit.

Geoff handed over the box with a cocky, satisfied smile. "Which is it— me or the pizza?"

3

The only good thing about the face mask Avery wore was that it covered the blush she could feel spreading across her cheeks.

But she smelled like vinegar.

She looked like a cave monster.

And Geoff? He looked like the famous dating and relationship podcaster he was. His off-duty style was impeccable, from the T-shirt that hugged his seriously-toned biceps, to his slim-cut black denim. His thick, dark hair was perfectly styled, and just the right amount of stubble clung to his chiseled jaw.

"Geoff! What are you doing here?" Her eyes would have gone wide if the face mask hadn't prevented her from moving more than her lips. Instead, her voice went high-pitched and strangled.

Geoff winked at her like he was enjoying a joke. Probably at her expense. "Nice to see you, too, Cheese Girl."

Oh dammit.

Definitely at her expense.

Avery gritted her teeth as best as she could given the circumstances. "For the last time, Beeker is not the same as Beecher's Cheese." The local Seattle brand was famous for its flagship cheese, and the macaroni and cheese they sold at their Pike Place location was revered by celebrities including Oprah and Martha Stewart. "All you're doing is illustrating the importance of knowing how to spell."

She shifted the pizza box in her hands, the heat from the pie spreading onto her palms. "Speaking of spelling," she said, on a roll now, since apparently her self-defense mechanism was to babble like an idiot. Geoff's grin got wider, and she pressed on. "You know I love your mom, but I have to disagree with the way she spelled your name. Geoffrey? G-E-O-F-F instead of J-E-F-F?" She shook her head. "It's a travesty. Like you're a rock or something."

"Well, I am hard."

"Eww!" Sophie shrieked from the next room. "You're disgusting."

Avery bit back a smile. "The only thing hard is your head."

"If you say so, Cheese Girl."

She rolled her eyes. "You couldn't at least call me Dairy Queen or something?"

"I mean, I'd lick that cone."

Another shriek from Sophie, who appeared in the living room wielding a pie server in one hand and a stack of paper plates in the other. "Say one more chauvinistic comment, and I'm going to stab you in the eye."

Geoff shook his head slowly and lifted his hands. "I wouldn't put fratricide past you."

Sophie nodded. "I mean, I would become Mom and Dad's sole beneficiary. There's a financial incentive here."

Geoff grinned and crossed the room to gather his sister in a hug. While he was preoccupied, Avery did another quick scan of his body. She hadn't seen Geoff since he moved to New York after college to pursue his broadcast dreams, and that East Coast water must have done a body good. He looked broader, better, and even more confident than when he'd left Seattle six years ago.

Sophie grumbled but accepted Geoff's hug, then stepped back and dropped the paper plates onto her coffee table. "What the hell are you even doing here?"

Geoff pointed at the pizza box clutched in Avery's hands. "I'm bringing you pizza."

"Pizza that I paid for."

Avery needed to get as far away from the pizza and Geoff's attention as possible. She dropped the box on the edge of the coffee table and sank onto the couch, trying to avoid his gaze. She was still wearing the stupid face mask and her old, ratty sweatpants. For chrissakes, she wasn't even wearing a bra.

Geoff flopped onto the far end of the couch with a loose-limbed confidence and smiled at his sister. "I need you to teach me how to cook." He caught Sophie's skeptical look and held up his hands. "For the show. I was thinking an aphrodisiac cooking session would really hook in some of my listeners."

Sophie narrowed her eyes and her mouth puckered like she was sucking on lemons. "I'll consider it, but I'm against your show on principle."

"You have to say that because you're my sister."

"No, I have to say that because I'm a feminist. You're teaching dudes how to scam women."

Geoff shook his head, his voice earnest. "No, I'm not, squirt. I'm teaching men how to improve their dating skills. How to be more effective in conversation, dress, and the works, so they can convert more dating opportunities into long-term prospects."

"Convert prospects? Like love is an equation?" Sophie huffed a sigh. "You and women." She cocked her head and grinned at Avery. "With gems like that, it's no wonder he's still single."

Geoff crossed his arms, drawing attention to the sculpted muscles of his chest and arms. "My job is to show other single guys the way, okay? Being single myself makes me more relatable to my audience."

"If you say so." Sophie pointed back at Avery, and Avery squirmed against the couch cushions. "You know, if you really want a good show, you should ask Avery to be a guest. She's an industry expert."

Geoff coughed in surprise. "She is?"

They both swung their attention to Avery, and her face burst into flames.

She opened and closed her mouth.

Opened it again.

"You know, I'm just going to wash my face. Hold that thought."

Avery jumped up off the couch and ran.

CHAPTER 2

*A*very emerged from Sophie's bathroom ten minutes after she'd hauled ass out of the living room, her face scrubbed mostly clean but still red from whatever face mask she'd wiped off. She'd missed a spot of goop by her temple, and Geoff fought the urge to point it out to her. Still, it made him smile as she returned to her spot on the couch.

He caught a whiff of strawberries as Avery sank onto the seat next to him. She looked weirdly caught in time, her face older than he'd remembered, but her light brown hair pulled into the French braids she used to wear whenever she was over at his place for sleepovers with Sophie. He had the feeling that he could have caught her in the middle of the night anywhere, that he could have been eighteen again like when he'd met her, instead of twenty-eight.

Geoff set down the beer he'd pulled from Sophie's fridge and nudged Avery's shoulder, her skin hot against his. "What's all this talk about you being an industry expert?"

She tugged on the hem of her T-shirt, a thin number that did little to conceal the soft curves of her body. She blew out a breath and smiled up at him. "I'm on the PR team at X Enterprises."

"X Enterprises? The sex toy company?" He felt his mouth open, and his breath puffed out.

Avery sank her teeth into the tempting curve of her lower lip. "One and the same."

"So you get paid to talk about sex toys."

She lifted a hand. "Talk about them. Try them. Share them with the world."

If he would have had a sip of beer in his mouth, he would have spit it out by now. Holy shit. Avery Beeker, his little sister's best friend, had been hiding a sexy side all along.

Not that she was so little anymore. Avery had grown up in the time he'd been gone. In New York, everyone was all about business, and everything Geoff had done was about, well, converting opportunities. But Avery was all Seattle-warm eyes, a laughing mouth, a runaround way of talking where you got a glimpse into her brain.

Maybe being back in Seattle was going to work out all right after all.

"Maybe Avery can help you," Sophie suggested. "You know, do a show about sex toys."

Avery Beeker and sex toys. God, that sounded like one of his high school wet dreams come to life.

Geoff brought his eyes to Avery's, her warm brown gaze ringed by long lashes. "So, what would you suggest?"

She pursed her lips. "That depends on what thesis you'd like to work with."

"Have you listened to the show before?"

The color of her cheeks deepened, and she dropped her eyes. "You should probably tell me about it. Who's your audience?"

Geoff grinned. If she hadn't heard too much from Sophie, maybe there'd be a chance for her to understand where he was coming from without jumping on the Geoff's-a-male-pig train. "*How to Hook a Hottie* is a dating and relationship show for men eighteen to thirty-five years old. Unlike Sophie seems to think, it's not about teaching guys to scam women. It's about helping them gain the skills and confidence to have more successful, fulfilling love lives."

Avery raised an eyebrow. "Does that mean getting laid more often?"

Well, shit.

His cock twitched at the suggestion in her voice. Geoff cleared his throat and adjusted his pants. "I'm not going to lie, that's a great end result. But it's also about having a great relationship. I bring in industry experts to help with everything from verbal and nonverbal communication to executing great dates. People like relationship therapists, sex therapists, and even event planners."

"So you're a jack of all trades?"

"Kind of. But if you work for a sex toy company…"

Avery tapped a finger to her lips. "Maybe we could do a segment on the benefits of using toys with a partner."

"That would be great." Geoff drummed his fingers on his knees. "And maybe to add a twist, you could also cover the how and when to introduce sex toys in the first place."

Was it him, or did her face get even more red?

Avery fiddled with the hem of her shirt again. "Yes, we could make that happen." She frowned. "Probably." She caught his eye, and a warm feeling spread through his chest. "I'd need to run everything by my boss. Get approval and make sure this fits into our long-term marketing plans."

"Right." He nodded. "Makes sense."

"Just don't let him change you into a player like him," Sophie warned.

Geoff's jaw tightened. Nothing like a little sister to throw you under the bus. "I'm not a player."

Sophie rolled her eyes. "Right. You're helping people."

Avery nodded and caught his eye. "In fairness, if you're helping people, I guess I am too." She took on a teasing tone. "At the end of the day, it's all about pleasure, right?"

Geoff grinned, his chest lightening. "Right. I'm pro-pleasure, and that makes me pro-sex toys, too."

Avery laughed, and Geoff reached for one of the beers he'd set on the table and offered it to her. She cracked it open and wrapped her lips around the mouth, her neck long and graceful as she swallowed.

Geoff tore his gaze away, back to the screen where Chris Hemsworth's face was frozen in a grimace. "Anyway," he continued, cutting his eyes at Sophie, "maybe Avery will be the one to corrupt me."

Beside him, Avery choked on a swallow of beer as his sister muttered, "Unlikely."

Avery tried to recover, pulling herself back together and dabbing at her mouth with the back of her hand. She set her beer on the table and slid the pizza box closer to her. "So, who's hungry?"

"Me!" Sophie crowed.

"Geoff?" Avery didn't meet his eye as she opened the lid. "Are you in or are you out?"

The smell of sauce and cheese wafted through the room, and Geoff's stomach growled.

Why the hell not?

He grinned and reached for a plate. "Well, since you both asked so nicely, I'll stay."

CHAPTER 3

"*A*re you spying on the morning production meeting?"

Avery pulled her eyes away from the conference room that she—yep, definitely—had been peering into, and whirled to face the source of the sing-song voice. "Naomi! What are you doing here?" Her heart skittered in her chest.

The X Enterprises receptionist lifted her coffee cup and grinned. "It's almost ten, and I'm still at least a cup of coffee short of my ideal caffeination level." She reached for the break room's coffee pot and filled her mug. Then she turned and narrowed her eyes at Avery. "Like I said, are you spying?"

Avery's cheeks flushed. "Nope. I just need to catch Jeremy before he gets pulled into another meeting."

"You might want to work on your subtlety." Naomi gestured over Avery's shoulder at the clear glass walls of the conference room. "That being said, your timing might have worked out in your favor."

The X Enterprises headquarters in downtown Seattle was a case study in perfect branding. The offices dominated the top floor of one of the tallest buildings in the city, and everything about them screamed *sex appeal*, from the dark marble floors and the sleek, tasteful portraits of nudes hung gallery-style along the hallways, to the interior glass walls that allowed natural light to stream in. The glass also provided convenient opportunities to check in on the whereabouts of your coworkers. If you could be smooth about it.

Avery followed Naomi's gaze to the conference room, where the morning meeting seemed to be adjourning. Her coworkers in Sales and Accounting moved toward the door, notebooks and pens in hand.

"Thanks, Naomi," Avery said. "Are we still on for lunch?"

Naomi nodded, and Avery lifted her coffee cup and stepped out into the hall. She intercepted Jeremy Glass, the X Enterprises founder and CEO, just before he made it into his corner office.

"Jeremy, do you have a quick second? I had a new PR opportunity I wanted to run by you." Avery clutched her coffee cup, grateful for the steadying warmth of the ceramic. She'd always liked Jeremy, but between his power and his good looks, he could be kind of intimidating at times.

Jeremy's handsome face brightened, and he raked a hand through his dark blond locks. "Actually, I'm glad you stopped me. I have something I wanted to discuss with you as well." He glanced at his wristwatch, an expensive-looking hunk of platinum. "I've got about twenty minutes now, as long as you don't mind me making a quick phone call first."

"Yeah, sure."

Jeremy waved her into his office and gestured for her to sit in one of the executive chairs across the desk from him.

Avery perched on the edge of the chair and set her cup down on the wide, wood surface of his desk while he reached for his phone.

"Vanessa? Any chance you can join me and Avery in my office?" Jeremy grinned. "Yes. About that thing."

Avery's stomach knotted. Vanessa, Jeremy's fiancée, was the head of the charity contributions committee, but Avery couldn't imagine what the two of them would need to talk to her about together.

Jeremy returned the phone to its cradle and smiled at her. "While we're waiting for Vanessa, tell me what you have."

Avery cleared her throat, her heart thumping. "Right. Well, I ran into an old friend this weekend, and he happens to be the personality behind

How to Hook a Hottie. It's a podcast for men in our target demographic, and the show is all about giving the audience tips and tricks for improving your love life. My friend invited me to be on the show as an industry expert, and I suggested we discuss the ways that using sex toys with a partner can benefit your relationship."

Jeremy nodded, a smile on his face. "I like where you're going with this, Avery. I think it's a great idea."

"You do?" She sat back in her chair, caught between excitement that she'd impressed Jeremy and a little dread. She'd secretly been hoping that Jeremy would say no and let her off the hook. Because getting on the air with Geoff could be a recipe for disaster, given that she could barely think straight around him, let alone talk.

But now she was in it.

"I do."

Goody.

"Great," she said, her voice weak. "But are you sure it shouldn't be Everett? He's awesome at promoting user experiences."

Jeremy shook his head. "No, it should be you. You're the one with the connection. That camaraderie will be great." He rapped his knuckles on the edge of his desk. "I'll even have Vanessa wrangle up a bunch of toys for you to bring along."

"What am I bringing?" a teasing voice asked from the doorway.

Avery turned in her chair as Vanessa Reese entered the office and closed the door behind her. Petite and dark-haired with kind eyes, Vanessa was a powerhouse of a woman—one apparently strong enough to bring even Jeremy Glass to his knees. The diamond ring he'd given her last January sparkled on her finger, a reminder that happily ever after was possible, even with an against-the-rules office romance.

Jeremy smiled at his fiancée. "Avery just pitched me a podcast opportunity where she'll go on air to promote some of our toys. If you can find a bunch of couple-friendly ones, that would be great."

Vanessa nodded and sank into the chair next to Avery. "I'm on it." She turned to Avery. "You've really been kicking butt on the whole marketing thing, and Jeremy and I wanted to say thank you."

Avery's mouth flopped open. "Yeah, of course. I love my job."

Vanessa grinned. "Good, because we were hoping you might be able to help out on another assignment."

"Oh?" Avery sat forward in her seat. "Do we have a new announcement for the charity contributions branch? Or a new product to unveil?"

Vanessa and Jeremy exchanged a glance, and Jeremy cleared his throat. "Actually, it's something a little more personal." He rubbed a thumb over his lower lip, and a crease formed between his eyes. "I'm not sure how much you were aware of it, but when word of our engagement was announced, it became something of a media firestorm."

Avery winced. She'd seen the magazine headlines—*X Enterprises CEO to wed employee*. And some of the less forgiving ones—*Can this sweet social worker tame the infamous sex toy CEO? Let's hope this marriage doesn't crash and burn.*

Media firestorm was a nice way to put it. Avery would have said *shit show.*

"I saw a few things," she hedged.

Jeremy nodded. "We'd like to do things a little differently when we announce the wedding."

Vanessa laughed lightly. "We didn't quite anticipate how many people would care about our engagement. We're hoping you can help us draft an announcement that will satisfy the press but let us maintain a little privacy as well."

Avery nodded, her chest light. "I can do that. Are you going to announce a wedding date?"

"No." Vanessa shook her head. "We'll send the announcement to the press the day before, but that's it. Nothing so far in advance that we'll get too much attention. We want to do a fairly quiet ceremony and reception where our friends and family can enjoy each other without worrying about a media circus."

"Sounds perfect." Avery smiled at Jeremy and Vanessa. "I'll run everything by you, but I'd be happy to help."

"Thank you." Vanessa's face softened. "And Avery, the invites aren't out yet, but we'd love it if you'd come. As far as guests from the office go, it'll be mostly managers, but you'd have a big part in this day."

Avery couldn't help the way her smile grew. "Really?" Hell yes, sign her up for a fancy wedding. There was nothing like a solid party to make her feel like all was right in the world. Vanessa nodded, and Avery pressed a hand to her chest. "I'd be honored."

They wrapped up a few details, and Vanessa promised to bring a few toys to Avery for Geoff's show. Then Avery slipped back to her desk, her stride confident as she made her way through the glass hallways. Her job really was the best, and days like today made her feel like she could take on the world.

Avery dropped into her chair, and her phone buzzed with an incoming text message. She reached for it, and her pulse quickened when she saw Geoff's name appear on the screen. Despite the fact that she'd known him for ten years, their relationship had always been a periphery one. She'd met Sophie freshman year of high school when Geoff was already a senior, but she was Sophie's best friend. Geoff may have been Sophie's brother, but Avery and Geoff had never exchanged contact information until this past weekend.

Avery's fingers had burned when she'd handed Geoff her phone to enter in his phone number and email address, and her face had heated when he slipped on that lazy, confident grin.

Hey, Cheese Girl, I was just working on my content calendar, he sent now. *Any luck running things by your boss?*

Still Cheese Girl? she texted back.

Should I call you Vibrator Girl instead?

She groaned. *You could try Avery.*

That's got a nice ring to it. She could picture Geoff's grin, and her stomach fluttered. *So, Avery?* he wrote. *Any luck?*

She blew out a deep breath. *Actually, yes. You have perfect timing. I got the thumb's up, and we're on.*

Great. I usually record on Wednesdays. Can you carve out some time for me this week?

Avery swallowed a spike of panic. She was so much better at writing press releases than doing on-air interviews. Writing was easy. On paper, you got do-overs. In real life, not so much. In real life, when you told a guy you were thirsty, he didn't think you wanted a drink of water, he thought you were desperate for his junk.

Avery sighed and typed her reply. *I'll make it happen.* She had to. Jeremy had insisted.

CHAPTER 4

*T*he doorbell rang, and Geoff forced himself to wait an extra minute before answering it, trying to hide the fact that he'd been sweating and staring at the door for the last ten minutes. Seeing Avery again shouldn't have made him so agitated, but he was. Maybe because Avery now was somehow so different from Avery back in high school. But also kind of the same in all the best ways.

He swung open his apartment door and smiled. "Avery, you made it. Cheese Girl strikes again."

She rolled her eyes. "Careful, Rock. Call me that again, and Cheese Girl might strike with her hands and not just her mouth."

He grinned. "I wouldn't mind if you struck with your mouth."

She groaned, but her eyes sparkled with amusement. "And to think, there are girls who fall for this."

"It's nice to see you too, Ave." Geoff leaned around the giant box she was carrying to hug her, and his body sparked at the touch. She was soft and warm against his skin, and when he bent closer to whisper in her ear, her shampoo smelled like strawberries. "But you've been spending too much time around my sister."

Avery stepped back, the blush of her cheeks ever so slightly warmer in

17

color than her makeup. Making her squirm was just as much fun as he remembered.

Avery cleared her throat and tightened her grip on the box. "Don't worry—I like to form my own opinions. I'll give you the benefit of the doubt if you behave."

"I appreciate that, Cheese Girl."

"Cheese Girl again? I'm not taking the bait." She shook her head with a smile. "So, what's the game plan, Rock?"

"You should probably show me what's in the box, and then we'll dive right in." Geoff cocked his head at her, surveying her form-fitting gray dress and high heels. She looked good. Professional but sexy as hell. "You're still okay with the fact that we live-stream the video feed at the same time that we record the audio, right?"

Avery nodded. "I appreciate the head's up on that. Wouldn't have wanted to show up in my old college sweatshirt."

"Go, Travelers."

She brightened. "You remembered I went to USC?"

"How could I not? I was jealous of all that sunshine." He'd never admit it to her, but Geoff had thought about Avery in California a lot in the years he'd lived on the East Coast, especially on days when New York was covered in enough snow to make him question why the hell he'd ended up there. She seemed like the only smart one among them, escaping to adventures in warm, sunny places, although now they were both back in the Seattle gloom, so there was that.

Avery grinned at him, and he took the box from her hands. "Let's go get started," he said.

Geoff led Avery through his apartment, and behind him, she let out a low whistle.

"Nice place."

He glanced around the apartment. "I've only been here for a few weeks, so I'm not totally unpacked yet. But thanks. It's got two bedrooms. One for me, one for my studio."

"Wow. Looks like you're really moving up in life."

He caught her eye and smiled. "Yeah, well, after my shoebox of an apartment in New York, anything would be an improvement."

He cracked open the studio door and set Avery's box of sex toys on the desk that took over the far wall of the room. He'd angled the desk to face out the window so he'd have the benefit of natural lighting for the video portion of his podcast. The view from his Capitol Hill apartment never got old—from here he could see not only the leafy, tree-lined streets of his neighborhood but all the way to downtown Seattle, where huge, glistening buildings stretched into the sky. At night the panorama glittered, and when he added in the fact that he could walk to everything from bars and restaurants to the grocery store, it just sweetened the deal.

Geoff pulled out a chair for Avery, and she sat down, smoothing the skirt of her dress. "Okay, Mrs. Claus, what did you bring me?" he asked.

She grinned and reached into her box. She pulled out a few silicone vibrators, and the sight of her holding a bunch of sex toys made his lips part. Definitely not his little sister's best friend. She was so much more.

"We've got a few toys for couples—a remote-controlled vibrator for fun out on the town, an insertable vibrator that a woman can wear during intercourse, and of course a cock ring or two."

Geoff licked his lips, his throat dry. "Of course." He shrugged like it was an everyday thing to have a beautiful woman giving him the run-down on adult products.

He rolled out the desk chair next to Avery's and sat down, waking his computer. While his recording program loaded on the screen, he grabbed a pair of recording headphones and moved back toward Avery.

"May I?"

She nodded, and he lowered the headphones onto her ears. He caught the way she sucked in a quick breath, and he smiled to himself.

"Are we good?" Geoff held up a thumb's up sign and grinned as she flashed the okay back at him.

He pulled on his own headphones and sat down next to her. Then he turned on the preview window to see what the video feed would display.

"Normally my guests are remote," he explained, "so I tend to do most of the video over Skype. But since you're here, let's see if we can fit in the same frame."

He pulled his chair closer to hers, and her slim shoulders—exposed in her sleeveless dress—brushed against his.

A wave of heat ran through him.

This would do.

Geoff adjusted the camera until the screen showed both of them, side by side. He and Avery looked good together, her brown eyes and delicate features a compliment to his dark coloring, her feminine curves a contrast to the muscle he'd earned through years of Crossfit workouts.

"You ready?"

She sucked in a breath and smiled. "Let's do it. *This*. Let's do *this*. The podcast." She slapped a hand over her mouth and blushed.

This was going to be fun.

Geoff cued the intro music, and it piped through their headphones. As it faded out, he began speaking. "Ladies and gentlemen, friends near and far, welcome back to *How to Hook a Hottie*. This week I'm joined by special guest, Avery Beech—" He caught himself about to use her Cheese Girl name, and she bit back a grin. He cleared his throat. "Miss Avery Beeker. She's the PR guru over at X Enterprises, one of the hottest adult products manufacturers in the country."

"In the world, actually," she said with a wink for the camera.

He swallowed his surprise. "I stand corrected. In the world. Today Avery's going to talk with us about how and when to introduce sex toys in your relationship. Avery, can you tell us a little about who you are and how you got to where you are today?"

She smiled. "First of all, thanks for having me on the show. As you mentioned, I'm the PR specialist for X Enterprises. I've been with the company ever since I got out of college, and it's been incredible to be a part of growing the awareness about the use of sex toys. I think a lot of people tend to put them into the category of things they don't talk about, but using sex toys and other adult products is a normal, healthy way to explore your sexuality, whether on your own or with a partner. The more pleasure you experience, the more you also get to take advantage of the side effects, like lowered heart rate and blood pressure, and reduced stress."

Geoff shook his head with a smile. "You heard it here first, friends. Get busy for your health."

"That's right." Avery's face lit. "And add some sex toys to spice it up."

"So, Avery, what have you brought to show us today?"

"Only the best, of course." She grinned and reached into the box.

GEOFF CLICKED the screen on his computer at the show's midpoint, rolling the advertisement from this week's sponsor, Slay All Night, a singles hookup app that promised the night of your fantasies with no strings attached.

He nudged Avery's shoulder. "That was awesome."

"Thank you."

She'd just completed a run-down of all the toys she'd brought to share, and he could see commenters on the live-stream already chiming in.

She's hot, from Alex37503.

Take me to bed, Avery, from IBeJohnson4U.

I'd play with her sex toys any day.

Okay, yeah, so a lot of his audience were pigs. But they could be princes in training if they'd just pay attention.

Avery cracked open a bottle of water and took a swig, wetting her pretty lips.

"You just about ready?" he asked, and she nodded.

She returned the bottle to the desk and smiled back at the camera.

Geoff faded out the sponsor's message and spoke. "Welcome back, friends. As you know, Avery and I were just talking about the benefits of using sex toys, and she showed us a few of her favorite products for couples." He turned to her. "Now I want to get into the nitty-gritty. When do you recommend introducing sex toys within a relationship?"

Avery's cheeks colored. "You know, I think that depends on each individual couple and your comfort level together. While more and more people discover sex toys each day, you want to be at a point where you're at least intimately acquainted with each other."

"So not on the first date?" he teased.

She shook her head. "Just like any sexual preference, you wouldn't start out on the first date by saying, 'Hey, I'm into sex toys.' First, you'd figure out if you like each other enough to even hop into bed together. Then, over time, you might start to explore some toys together."

"What about by the third date?"

Avery frowned. "Why that one in particular?"

"Well, I've got a theory that if you structure them correctly, within three dates you can know whether or not you'd like to have a relationship with that person. And, you know, the third date is often pretty critical for a couple."

She raised an eyebrow. "Oh yeah? I'd like to hear this theory."

"Let's do it. I like a challenge." Geoff rubbed his hands together and leaned closer to the camera. "My theory is that you can set up your dates to be kind of like the three acts in a traditional story."

Avery's eyes brightened, and she grinned. "The English major in you comes out."

"Shh," Geoff teased back. "I tell everyone I went to the school of Hard Knocks."

She rolled her eyes. "So, back to your three dates."

"Yeah, so date one is like Act One. It's the setup. You establish who the other person is, the boundaries of your attraction, and that person's world. There's a story question that gets raised, which in this case is, 'will we or won't we fall in love?'"

"Okay, I see where you're going with this."

Geoff smiled. "Date two, Act Two: the confrontation." Avery laughed, and he continued. "I don't mean there's a physical fight here, but this date is where you gather information about the other person to see how they act in a challenging situation. You can find out so much more about a person through how they act rather than what they say. I always recommend an active date—a cooking class or ice skating or something."

"Bungee jumping?"

Geoff laughed. "I'd say that's on the extreme end, but sure. And that brings us to date three, Act Three: the resolution. You know by now who the other person is, whether you can work well together to solve a problem. Now you need to decide if you're going to continue seeing each other or not. This is why the third date is usually so critical for a couple, and why so many people who decide 'yes' end up sleeping together for the first time."

Avery pursed her lips. "Hmm. That's a nice theory."

"You don't agree?" He took a swig from his water bottle.

She shrugged. "I mean, I might if I've ever gotten to the third date."

Geoff choked on his drink, spitting out a stream of water onto his keyboard.

Holy shit.

He coughed and tried to recover. "Ladies and gentlemen, for those of you who aren't watching the live-stream, I just spit my drink onto my desk." He looked at Avery, flabbergasted. "You've never had three dates with the same guy?"

"Rub it in, why don't you?" Her voice was light, but there was a bit of strain around her mouth, and her cheeks were pink again.

"Sorry, it's just that I'm trying to wrap my mind around this." He cleared his throat. "For those of you who can't see, I'm going to try to describe Avery to you and see if I can do her justice. She's got a face and body to bring a man to his knees and a mouth that could finish him off. Since she works for X Enterprises, I'll bet she's got the dirty-talk skills of a porn star." He searched her eyes as he spoke, proud of the way her eyes widened and her mouth fell open, that endearing blush creeping across her cheeks. "But aside from that, she's funny and kind. The kind of girl your mom wants you to date but who's also the kind of girl your friends are jealous you landed. She's the full package."

"Go on," Avery said, teasing. "Maybe you should write my dating profile for me." She leaned forward, her lips parted slightly. "Actually, I have an even better idea." She flashed him a shy smile and fisted her hands in her lap. "Why don't you give me one-on-one pointers to show me where I'm going wrong?"

"You mean take you out on three dates?"

She blushed deeper and lifted a shoulder. "Or I take you out. Yeah. Like, fake dates. Take me out, see what happens. You do what you would do, I do what I would do, and you give me pointers where I'm messing up."

Goosebumps raced along Geoff's skin. He'd always liked Avery, but thanks to Sophie, she'd always been off-limits before now. But Avery's challenge had just changed the game.

Thank god his sister refused to listen to his show because she was going to kill him for what he was about to do. Geoff licked his lips and smiled back at Avery.

"Yeah," he said, and then he echoed her earlier line. "Three dates. Let's do it."

CHAPTER 5

The September air had a brisk bite to it as Avery stood in front of Pike Place Fish Market, watching the vendors toss a fish back and forth before settling it into the crushed ice of the store's display case. An eager weekend crowd swarmed the aisles of the long-standing farmer's market, baskets and huge, colorful bouquets tucked under their arms.

The air smelled like the ocean and, more faintly, like fresh food and flowers. In the background, a busker sang the familiar strains of *You've Got To Hide Your Love Away*, glittery strands of Mardi Gras beads wrapped around the neck of his guitar.

"Hey." A warm hand landed on her shoulder and squeezed, and she turned to find Geoff grinning at her. He wore a button-down shirt that hugged the sculpted muscles of his chest, and his dark eyes smiled as they caressed her face.

"Hey," she whispered back. Her throat went dry, and her palms started to sweat.

Geoff looked the kind of good where she was going to blurt out another inappropriate remark and put her foot in her mouth once more. By this point, she was intimately acquainted with the taste of Gucci leather. Frankly, it wasn't that appetizing.

The fact that on his show she'd admitted she hadn't had three dates in a row with the same person, pretty much undermining all her credibility as an industry expert? The fact that she'd asked him out on air? Yeah, that had gone over really well with her boss.

"Maybe you shouldn't follow through on the date thing," Jeremy had advised gently on Thursday morning.

But she'd assured him that she knew what she was doing, and here she was anyway, on date number one. A glutton for punishment. And a liar, too. Avery didn't have a clue what she was doing here. Only that Geoff was hot and single and that maybe fake-dating him could help her put her high school crush on him to bed.

But not literally to bed.

Except...maybe? Trading in her V-card for a night with Geoffrey Carter wouldn't be the worst thing in the world. Other than the fact that Sophie would kill her.

Dammit.

Avery sighed and tightened her fingers around the strap of her purse. She couldn't even think straight around him.

"It's nice to see you," Geoff said.

"You too." She was going really smooth with all the words now. Ugh. She tilted her head and peered up at him. "So how's this whole thing supposed to work?"

Geoff grinned. "This date, you mean?"

Avery's stomach tightened. "Yeah. Are we pretending this is a real date, or is it a real date? Do I pretend we're strangers?"

"How about casual acquaintances who are exploring their long-standing attraction to one another?" The way he said it, dead-serious and deeply sexy, made her mouth drop open.

Oh shit.

Is that what this was? Because her pulse quickened and heat coiled in her belly in agreement. Why was it so hard to know which way was up?

"We pack our fish to travel! Airplane friendly!" called the vendor at the fish market.

The interruption broke Avery's trance, and she took a steadying breath.

Either way, standing here and catching flies in her mouth wasn't going to impress Geoff. She looked back up at him. "We can do that. And you'll tell me where I'm going wrong?"

He shrugged. "If you'd like." He nodded his chin toward the seafood display. "I don't mean to crush your hopes and dreams, but it smells like fish. Up for taking a stroll?"

Avery nodded in relief and started walking into the covered Pavillion section of Pike Place Public Market. "Let's go."

Geoff moved next to her and bumped her shoulder with his, sending heat through her body. "Good call on the date location."

She grinned. "If I recall, you suggested a causal, no-pressure first date. A low-key affair where you can continue on to another event if things go well."

His smile made her stomach flip. "Like coffee you can extend to lunch."

She nodded back. "Or drinks you can extend to dinner."

"Were you taking notes?" When Geoff grinned, a dimple appeared in his cheek. God help her.

"I might have been."

"Well," he said, "I approve."

Avery did a fake curtsey, and a tourist walking past bumped into her. Avery pitched forward, falling against Geoff's broad chest.

Oh.

Avery's body tingled every place she touched him, from his toned torso (hard) to his firm arms (strong), to the hands steadying her hips (surprisingly warm, but still commanding). She breathed him in as he set her back on her feet, bereft when he moved his hands from her sides.

Geoff swept his eyes down her body, bringing a rush of heat to her skin. His gaze landed on her high-heeled booties, and he chuckled. "What are you doing in those shoes, Ave?"

She lifted her chin and pushed back her shoulders. This was Geoff here. She needed to stop being stupid. "Channeling a gazelle."

His gaze darkened. "If you're a gazelle, you're the kind that gets taken out by a lion."

"Taken out?" A tiny breath puffed out of her. "Oh."

"And by taken out, I mean eaten."

Right.

Avery gritted her teeth and kept walking through the crowd, weaving past a colorful variety of vendors. On her right, she passed a stand selling homemade pasta, and still more stands boasted a riot of seasonal produce. "These shoes are sexy."

So was the rest of her outfit—skinny black jeans and a silky, lace-trimmed camisole topped by a featherweight cardigan. She'd worn her hair down around her shoulders in softly styled waves that screamed, *Touch me! Tangle your hands in me and pull me close!*

In theory.

Geoff weighed out his answer, his eyes amused. "They're hot shoes. But for today, you probably shouldn't have worn them. Do you even like them?"

Avery frowned at him and accepted the slice of Gala apple that a produce vendor offered her. "I like the way they look. I don't know if I love walking in them. But I don't get it. Shouldn't you be telling me to up the sex appeal?" She crunched the apple between her teeth, the sweet, bright flavor a balm against his words.

"Yes, if your goal is to have sex. But if your goal is to see if you can have a relationship, you need to focus on how to be authentically sexy."

She forced herself not to pout. Her goal was to have a relationship so she could have sex. Couldn't it go both ways? "I didn't know there was a difference. And isn't the whole point that pretty packaging helps get a guy interested enough to look closer? Then you get to be interested in other features."

"Yes. But you need to be authentic from the start. Sure, curl your hair or whatever. But there's a difference between hookups and love. My theory's about love."

Avery narrowed her eyes at him. "Have you ever been in love?"

"Ah. The sticking point." Geoff darted his eyes away and ignored the question. "Think of it this way. You know how Gwen Stefani has a signature red lip?"

Avery looked up at him, her own red lips pursed. "Oh my god, Geoff. Are you about to use a makeup analogy with me?"

He grinned. "Don't get too excited. My point is that lipstick is kind of her. But do you think she wears it to bed?"

"Unlikely."

"Right. So the people she goes to bed with need to be able to look at her without the makeup and not get shell-shocked."

"And you're saying I'm like Gwen Stefani?"

Geoff shrugged. "I'm just asking what the hell happened to the girl who sang the Spice Girls at my house all the time."

Avery blushed. "That was a stupid phase." It was a long phase, actually, filled with dorky music like *Wannabe* and *Say You'll Be There*. She wasn't proud of it.

"You don't need to apologize for the things you like."

"The things I like aren't always cool."

"As long as they're you, who the hell cares?" Geoff's voice was earnest, brimming with possibility, and it made her stop and consider.

"Authentically sexy," Avery repeated.

"Exactly."

"That's very deep of you," she teased.

He flashed her a rakish grin. "I do like to go deep."

"Geoff!" She pushed his arm and blushed, then drew a deep breath. "See, I thought we were going to have a moment there. But you ruined it."

He shot her another smile that pulled straight to her stomach and made it dip. "So about your lips..."

His teasing suggestion made her blush deeper. "What about them?"

He leaned in so close she feel the heat radiating off his skin, and her body involuntarily swayed forward, permitting her a whiff of his spicy, warm cologne. "Just like you, they're absolutely gorgeous." He lowered his voice until the seductive note scraped like a bow across a violin. "But they're entirely unkissable."

What?

Avery stumbled back from him, her shoulders tight. She scrunched her face. "What the hell, Geoff?"

He grinned again. "They're intimidating."

"They're stylish."

Geoff straightened to his full height, and she was suddenly aware of how masculine he was—all firm muscles and controlled energy. "Here's the thing about guys. We're base creatures, at the heart of things. Sure, we might want to have long-lasting relationships, but there's got to be an initial physical reaction. And while those lips are attractive, it's kind of tough to figure out how to kiss you. It'll break a guy's brain. Meaning he'll potentially give up a good thing just because it's exhausting."

Avery stopped short of pressing her fingers to her lips. Geoff was right. Even she didn't want to touch them.

Dammit.

"Okay. Point taken." They were nearing the end of the Pavillion, and the door to the exterior market lay ahead. Geoff led the way through the swarming crowd as they stepped back out into the crisp autumn air. Midday sun warmed Avery's shoulders, and a slight breeze wafted the scent of food vendors from the surrounding blocks.

Her stomach growled, and she nudged Geoff. "I have a secret motive for choosing Pike Place for today's date."

"You do, huh?"

She gestured at the building on the corner of Pike and Pine, and his gaze moved to the sign hanging above the shop's doorway.

"Beecher's."

Avery nodded. "Mac and cheese. So you can learn the distinct difference between my name and theirs."

"I applaud your effort. But I'm not really a mac and cheese kind of guy."

She stopped short on the sidewalk. "Excuse me?"

Geoff tried to shrug it off, but she wasn't buying his nonchalance. "I don't eat mac and cheese. Only the kind in the blue box."

A laugh burst from her throat. "You're kidding me."

He shook his head. "Nope."

"Are you six years old?"

He rubbed a hand over his chest. "I mean, what guy isn't, at heart?"

"Oh no." Avery grabbed his arm and smiled. "We're going in."

"There's a line." Geoff waved at the group of people crammed into the storefront and spilling down the buckled sidewalks.

"Sure is." She tugged his elbow. "Let's go."

Avery took another step forward, and her heel caught on one of the cobblestones lining the street. At least this time when she fell she was able to catch herself on Geoff's arm.

Avery steadied herself and jumped back, but Geoff caught her by the hand. A thousand sparks shot up her arm.

"About the shoes," he said.

She bit her lip. "Right. Dangerous." She met his eye, and her stomach dipped. "But also, I don't have a problem being in your arms right now."

Geoff's eyes widened, and she scolded herself internally. *Too much. Too aggressive.*

But he just laughed. "I see, it's all part of your plan."

She nodded, her chest loosening. "Exactly. Since you've already shown you're a nice guy, now you can't turn down my mac and cheese request."

"That's definitely one approach." His eyes crinkled at the corners when he smiled. "Still not going to work."

Avery leaned forward, daring herself to bring her lips close to his ear. "Tell you what—I'll make you a deal. I'll take off the lipstick and heels if you try some mac and cheese. Get us both out of our comfort zone."

She leaned back far enough to catch his wicked grin, and then lifted a finger to stop him. "Don't say anything about your comfort zones."

"Fine," Geoff said. "Anyway, you can't possibly walk around Pike Place barefoot, so I'll take your deal."

Avery bounced on her toes. "Yay! Let's get some food."

He shot a puzzled look at her, raking his eyes up and down her body. "What? *No.* You can't possibly have another pair of shoes on you."

She grinned and tugged his elbow again. "Wanna bet?"

CHAPTER 6

*A*very closed her lips around a forkful of Beecher's macaroni and cheese and grinned at Geoffrey. "See, I told you the mac and cheese was good."

He tilted his head to the side, a concession. "I admit defeat on this one." He raised a sauce-covered fork in her direction. "But I still say you lured me here under false pretenses."

"Muah-ha-ha," Avery chuckled, raising a pinky finger to the corner of her lips, Doctor Evil style. "A good ex-Girl Scout always comes prepared." She pointed down at her shoes, a pair of flats that she'd pulled from her purse twenty minutes ago. At first, Geoff hadn't believed the tiny pieces of leather could be shoes, but the fabric unfolded with some sort of witchery into a full-fledged pair of flats. Avery had shoved her booties into her purse and slipped on the tiny shoes. Somehow they transformed her, made her literally and metaphorically more grounded. She'd also swiped away the lipstick, leaving her lips stained pink but way more kissable. Not that he was noticing.

Geoff flicked his eyes away from Avery's mouth and caught her eye. Behind her, in the glass-enclosed room next to the eating area where they sat now, a Beecher's employee ran what looked like a rake through a tub of curds and whey bigger than three bathtubs put together.

Kind of gross, actually.

But letting Avery have this victory made Geoff's chest feel warm. He chewed the last bite of his food, wiped a napkin over his lips, and tossed the napkin, fork, and now-empty container of food into the trash.

Avery followed his lead, sliding off her seat to throw away her trash and then stepping out onto the street. A throng of people in blue and green Seattle Sounders gear trudged by with soda bottles clutched in their hands.

Geoff looked over his shoulder at Avery. "Is it game day?"

She followed his gaze and shrugged. "For the Sounders? Maybe."

He leaned back on his heels. "God, I haven't seen a Sounders game in years."

"No?" Avery cocked her head at him, her hair waving around her shoulders. It looked soft. Touchable.

"I was more of New York Yankees fan the last few years." The corners of his lips pulled down. "More by default than anything. But I missed soccer."

Avery giggled and started walking aimlessly up the street. "You're such a nerd."

Geoff jogged to catch up with her, admiring the way her ass swayed as she navigated the cobblestone street in her magic flats. "Watch who you're calling a nerd, Cheese Girl. That's a dating pointer."

She lifted an eyebrow at him. "Watch who you're calling Cheese Girl, Rock." She grinned and started crossing the street. "Also a pointer."

"Touché."

God, this girl. Once she stopped living in her head and worrying about how she looked, she was pretty damn funny.

The soft strains of an outdoor pianist's chords brightened the air and made anything seem possible. "What do you say we catch a game?" Geoff called out.

Avery paused on the far side of the street. "Really?"

"Yeah. I mean, if we can get tickets. Could be kind of fun." She looked at him, deciding, and he pressed. "If I recall, you were a soccer player back in high school, yourself."

Avery's voice was quiet. "I can't believe you remember that."

"Why? It wasn't that long ago."

She snorted. "We attended high school together for precisely one year before you shipped off to college, and you always seemed so caught up in your popular crowd events. I didn't think you noticed."

Geoff reached for her hand and squeezed, his throat thick. "Of course I noticed." He'd never let his attraction go anywhere, but that didn't stop it from being there to begin with. Didn't stop him from thinking about Avery long after he'd left for college, and then later New York.

Avery's chest rose with a deep breath, her breasts pushing up against the thin material of her silky camisole. "Okay," she said.

Geoff rubbed a thumb over the back of her hand. "Okay to me noticing or to the game?"

She lifted her eyes and smiled at him like a challenge. "In the spirit of getting out of my comfort zone, to both."

* * *

"Okay, I know we haven't even gone inside yet, but this day is kind of the best." Avery grinned up at Geoff, her hand gripping his arm as they walked toward CenturyLink Field. Seattle's sports stadium, home to today's Sounders soccer game, sat a little over a mile from Pike Place Market. As Geoff and Avery approached the outer gates, they joined streams of green-and-blue-clad soccer fans, and the air snapped with a kind of electricity that couldn't only be accounted to the upcoming game.

It felt nice to have Avery's hands on him—strange after years of not touching but also somehow comfortable, like they'd been doing this for a while.

"That's the cookie talking, Cheese."

Avery rolled her eyes. "Just take it as a compliment." She cocked her head. "Or maybe it's just me complimenting myself for planning a great date."

Geoff grinned. After he'd hopped on his phone to buy tickets to today's match (thanks, Internet), he and Avery had made the walk toward CenturyLink Field. As they strolled through the last block of Pike Place, a drift of air that smelled like ginger and molasses and sugar had washed over them.

Avery's eyes had grown huge as she peered into a bakery case that held cookies as big as her face.

"Gingerbread is my favorite." She'd looked like a puppy, and he'd wanted to feed her.

Geoff had whipped out his wallet and forked a fiver over to the girl behind the counter.

"Geoff, I shouldn't." Avery tugged his arm.

He'd clucked his disapproval. "Today's not about the rules, sweetheart. It's about authenticity. And if you authentically want the cookie, then you should have it."

She'd smiled, and he'd felt so proud. "Twist my arm, why don't you?"

Now Geoff was glad he'd insisted on the treat. They'd shared it, fingers brushing inside the paper bag, sugar on lips and skin, and his chest, at least, felt like soaring.

"A great date, huh?" he asked.

Avery blushed, and he pulled her into the nearest sports memorabilia store. Sounders and Mariners jerseys hung from the walls, and the store's shelves were crammed with everything from Sounders sunglasses to branded blankets and seat cushions.

"Our seats are going to be kind of high, so I'm guessing they'll be in the shady section," Geoff said, glancing at Avery's cardigan. She looked at him with a question in her eyes. "Meaning cold."

"Oh." She nodded. "Right."

"Let's get you a scarf." He pointed at a table display of scarves. "Pick one." Avery's eyes got big again, and he smiled. "Pretty sure you're the one who's six years old," he said. "Buy you a present, and you get so happy."

"Is that really so bad?" she asked.

Geoff rubbed a hand through his hair. "No, Ave, it's not."

She studied the display and selected a green and blue scarf with the Sounders logo stitched in bold, cheesy letters.

"That's the one?"

"Yep." Avery smiled as she headed toward the register. At the front of the line, she reached for her wallet, but Geoff stopped her with a hand on her arm.

"My treat."

She grinned even wider, and his face got hot. "Thank you."

"Of course."

Geoff paid for their purchase, and Avery wrapped the scarf around her neck. It clashed with her entire outfit, but it also put a grin on her face that made him want to smile, too.

They exited the shop and made their way through the stadium's security lines, grabbing two plastic cups of beer and locating their seats just as the clock counting down to game time hit five minutes. Despite Geoff's original concerns, the seats weren't bad after all. From here, he and Avery were high enough to get a full-field view from close to the midfield line, and to also see over the top of the stadium to where the Space Needle and Ferris Wheel scraped against the sky.

Avery dropped into her seat and settled her cup into the plastic cupholder attached to the chair in front of her. The air smelled like popcorn, hotdogs, and beer, and Geoff felt like he was twelve again. That was probably the last time they'd all gone to the game as a family—he and his parents and Sophie. After that came The Announcement, and then The Divorce, and then, well...

Avery nudged his arm, drawing him out of his thoughts. "Look at us, being all spontaneous."

He smiled back at her and swallowed a sip of his beer. "To getting out of our comfort zones."

Geoff settled against the plastic seat, and the cold bit through his jeans. Maybe he should have gotten a scarf for himself, too. Or he could just move closer to Avery. For body heat. It was simple thermodynamics.

He leaned his arm on their shared armrest, and before long, the infectious energy of the crowd swept him up and chased away the cold. He clapped and cheered along with Avery as the stadium's two large screens projected an image of a pretty girl stepping to the center of the field. She wore a glittery tiara in her hair and a Miss Seattle sash tied over her stylish trench coat.

Miss Seattle walked to the microphone and smiled to the crowd. "Scarves up, Seattle," she called, and the crowd stood, everyone with a Sounders scarf flashing their scarves back at her.

Beside him, Avery jumped to her feet, hooting and hollering as she lifted her new scarf.

As Miss Seattle ended her segment, Geoff gestured at Avery's scarf. "Aren't you glad you got that?"

She beamed at him and dropped back into her seat. "Thank you again." Over her shoulder, a flash of color filled the projection screen. Now the cameras panned from group to group, capturing a couple of kids in full-out face paint, a group of college-aged kids waving styrofoam fingers.

And then him and Avery.

Holy shit.

"Cheese, look." Geoff nudged Avery, and her face broke out into a huge smile of recognition. She lifted her hand to wave to the camera, and seeing her so happy made something inside him give. He wanted to make her that happy, too.

Before he could think twice, he reached a hand on either side of her face. The world narrowed down to Avery's pretty eyes, to her enticing lips falling open in a sweet gasp.

He leaned forward and captured her mouth with his, kissing her gently, breathlessly. She tasted like cinnamon, and she felt like home. His heart slammed in his chest as the crowd erupted around him, but he was here in this moment as Avery yielded to him, parting her lips and letting him taste her. Her hair fell over the backs of his hands like silk, and he tightened his grip, making her moan into his mouth.

Avery.

Oh, Jesus Christ.

When he finally pulled back, chest heaving, the camera had long since panned away.

But his sister's best friend just stared back at him, her eyes dazed, and a slow smile spreading on those definitely kissable lips.

Geoff sat back in his chair, all the cold replaced by fire in his veins. He might never be cold again.

Avery touched a finger to her mouth. "What was that for?" she whispered.

He grinned at her. "Kiss Cam."

She lifted an eyebrow like she could see right through him. "Consider me a fan."

CHAPTER 7

a giant bouquet of roses obscured Naomi's head on Monday morning, but there was no mistaking the glee in her voice as she carried the blooms through the X Enterprises office. "Special delivery!"

Avery's mouth dropped open as Naomi approached her desk, and she pressed a hand to her chest. "Are those for me?"

"They are, and they're heavy."

Avery swept a few papers on her desk into a neat stack, and Naomi settled the vase into the spot she'd cleared.

"You must really have impressed someone," Naomi said.

Avery forced her face to go neutral. "Guess so."

Naomi straightened and looked at her expectantly. "So? Who are they from?"

Avery reached for the small envelope the florist had tucked among the stems. Her fingers brushed the petals, and they released a sweet, heady fragrance that perfumed the air in the office.

She slid open the envelope and pulled out the simple card. It had only two words: *Go, Sounders.*

Avery blushed and touched her fingers to her lips. "Just a friend."

Just a friend who had kissed her like he meant it. Just a friend who'd made the whole world stop spinning for a moment of time.

She and Geoff hadn't talked about it for the rest of the game, but somehow their fingers kept touching, and they'd high-five for each one of the three goals the Sounders had scored. When the game let out, and the crowd swept down the stadium stairs in a frenzy, Geoff had wrapped his arms around her shoulders and pulled her against his side.

She'd told herself he was just being chivalrous and protecting her. But it had meant more to her than that.

And maybe it had to Geoff, too.

"I need more friends like yours," Naomi said with a knowing sparkle in her eye.

"Someone's trying to make me look bad," issued a deep male voice over Avery's shoulder.

Avery turned to smile at Jeremy. Her boss had always stocked the offices with fresh flowers, even keeping a table in the marble-and-glass women's room for the sole purpose of holding new blooms.

"You remember Geoffrey Carter from *How to Hook a Hottie?*" she asked.

Jeremy lifted an eyebrow. "Yes."

Oh shit, now what was she going to say? *Think, Avery.*

"We're exploring, um, partnership opportunities."

Her cheeks burned, but Jeremy just nodded. "Turning it around, are we?"

"Yep." Avery dropped her eyes to the flowers. "We are." Maybe she could use this to her advantage.

Jeremy and Naomi returned to their desks, and Avery reached for her cell phone and a notebook. She hugged them against her chest and hurried into the nearest empty conference room.

The bad thing about the open floor plan and glass walls? Anyone could see what you were doing. But at least with the conference room door closed, no one could hear her eat her words.

"Cheese Girl." Geoff's tease should have made her angry, but his honey-warm tone made something catch in her chest.

"Rock."

"You know, I kind of like when you call me that."

Avery grinned and cleared her throat. "I'm not sure what the protocol is for our, um, relationship, but I feel like you're going above and beyond here."

"You mean the flowers?"

She rubbed her free hand over her pencil skirt and lowered her voice. "I mean the flowers."

"They're all part of my plan, Cheese. You like them?"

"I love them." Avery glanced through the offices. Even from here, she could spot the bright wash of pink they loaned to the sleek space. "Thank you."

"You're welcome."

Avery blew out a breath. She still needed to figure out how to spin this to make sure her job wasn't in jeopardy. "So, I was talking to our CEO about partnership opportunities in the future."

"Mmm." Geoff's voice in her ear raised a few fantasies in her mind. "You know what that sounds like to me?"

She squirmed and pressed her thighs together. Her voice came out high and breathy. "What's that?"

"Like a second date."

It wasn't entirely what she'd had in mind, but it also wasn't a bad idea. "I like where you're going with this."

"Me too." She could hear Geoff moving around in the background—the shuffle of papers, some soft music coming from computer speakers. "Did you happen to visit any of the gossip websites this past weekend?" he asked.

Her chest tightened. "No. Why?"

"Because the video of us—you know, the one from the stadium—got picked up by TMZ."

Avery put him on speaker phone so she could pull up the website on her phone. Sure enough, a still from the video of the two of them at the game popped up on her screen—Geoff's hands in her hair, her eyes closed and one hand pressed against his chest, over his heart.

Seeing the photo sent tingles through her body, and the air sucked out of her lungs.

She looked so freaking happy, so blissfully absorbed in his kiss.

It had been a good kiss. A really good one.

But then she dropped her eyes lower and skimmed the caption underneath the photo. *Dating expert Geoffrey Carter and his latest conquest lock lips at the Sounders' winning match.*

Oh. Her stomach sank.

Image was everything. Avery knew it. She lived and breathed it, in her job and in her life. And she'd just gotten lumped into the same category as all the other girls who'd fallen for him. She'd spent enough time around Sophie to know exactly how stupid that made her seem.

"Do they know that I'm not your conquest?" Avery asked. "That this whole thing started on your show?"

Which was it—real or not real? Because the date may have been a setup, but the way the kiss felt had shifted everything for her.

"Who cares if TMZ does? My audience has been super responsive. I've had a ten percent boost in downloads this week, mostly focused on your episode."

Good for him.

Bad for her.

The more people that downloaded her disastrous episode and heard her talk about her dating failures, the more vulnerable it made her position at X Enterprises.

Avery reached for the phone with trembling fingers and turned off the speakerphone. She lifted the phone to her ear, and Geoffrey continued. "Let's keep it up, and we'll be in excellent shape going forward. This kind of exposure will really help me bring in more revenue from sponsors."

"Right, sponsors," she repeated back. Her lips felt numb.

This was all just a ploy for the show. That kiss—her happiness, the flowers—none of it had been real.

Avery's throat constricted, and her stomach knotted. She'd gotten too caught up in the adrenaline and the sugar rush, and she'd imagined a spark of something that didn't exist. That's what happened when she let go of the reins. She needed to get control again and figure out how to twist this in her favor, just like she'd promised Jeremy.

She straightened her spine and reached for the notebook she'd brought with her. "So back to our partnership opportunities." She clicked open her pen and steadied her voice. "Any ideas for date number two?"

"Actually, yes. Mind if I take a stab at planning this one?"

Avery sighed and clicked her pen closed. "Have at it."

CHAPTER 8

"*I* can't believe I've never done this before," Avery called over her shoulder, dipping a kayak oar into Lake Union. Her kayak pulled smoothly through the water as she passed the houseboats that crowded the lake. The view from up close rather from the highway made everything seem new and fresh, and Geoff hurried to catch up with her.

They'd taken advantage of the Indian summer weather for today's date, and the lake water sparked in the sunlight. Despite the fact that it was late September, the air warm was enough to wear just a bathing suit, and Geoff had to admit it was a definite perk.

Too bad the life preserver covered Avery's whole suit now.

"Me neither," Geoff said. "But I figured now that I'm back in Seattle, I should play tourist for a while. Catch up on all the things I overlooked when I was here."

He hoped she knew that included her.

How he'd let her slip through his fingers before when she'd been right under his nose was alarming, but he planned to make up for lost time.

All those excuses—being older, being her best friend's brother—seemed less important now than they had when they were younger. Geoff had told his audience all about it when he'd recorded his date wrap-up episode this past Wednesday. He just hadn't told Avery herself yet.

And he wouldn't until he knew it was real for her, too.

Avery softened a bit. "Tell me what you missed."

"Ah, so many things. Air without cigarette smoke—the kind that you can really fill your lungs with. Trees everywhere you look. Coffee so fresh and essential that it's almost part of your DNA."

Avery laughed, and Geoff stroked his paddle faster, speeding up his kayak to bring himself beside her. Light reflected off the tiny waves in the Sound, casting a warm glow on Avery's face. Geoff reached for the side of her boat and pulled her craft against his, holding it steady. They bobbed in the water, their boats rocking together and the sun on their shoulders.

"Is that why you moved back?" Avery asked. "The coffee?"

Geoff shrugged. "I originally thought I was going to go do broadcast shows in New York, but I started to realize I wanted to do my own thing instead of being stuck working for someone else. And that meant I could be anywhere, even back home."

"Is that why you started your show? Because you wanted your own thing?"

"That was a big part of it. But every day I'd walk through the streets for hours, just people-watching, you know? You can't get that anywhere else—all those bodies crammed together. And there were so many stories to tell."

Avery flashed him a warm, genuine smile. "There you go again, Mr. English Major."

Geoff ducked his head. "Yeah, yeah. Anyway, the stories that I kept wanting to tell were about people connecting with other people. In today's world, there are so many things shouting at you—your phone, the internet, your TV—that it's hard to quiet down enough to hear your own voice, let alone someone else's."

"And that's where you come in." Her voice was so quiet he could barely catch it above the waves.

"I didn't seek out the idea, Ave. It kind of came to me." Geoff sighed. "And I know that makes me seem like such a player, but it really is about helping other people find those connections."

A wistful look crossed her face. "Yeah, I get that. Is that when you developed your super awesome three-date formula?"

He shrugged, wary. "I guess so."

She gestured out at the lake. "So this still fits into your second-date philosophy, right?" Her mouth went flat. "Something full of adventure to see how you handle problems together?"

"Yeah, something like that."

The way she called it out made him uneasy. During their podcast recording he'd agreed to date her, only he hadn't expected it to be for more than the show when he said yes. But that kiss—man.

It was easier to couch it as a stunt for the show, but it didn't mean he felt any less strongly about her. She'd somehow managed to flip the whole way he saw her, and she wasn't just a friend anymore, but a real prospect.

"Are you still mad that the press called you my conquest?" he asked.

Avery's mouth tightened.

Bingo.

"You're not, you know. A conquest."

She lifted a single shoulder. "Well, that's good, I guess."

Fuck. "Is it?" he asked. He didn't know which way was up. Did she want to be a conquest or did she not?

Avery's face scrunched. "I mean, you tell me."

Geoff let go of her kayak and rubbed a hand over his face. Before he thought twice about it, he grabbed his kayak paddle and dashed it into the water, sending a huge splash of lake water onto her lap.

"What?!" Avery shrieked, sputtering. "You did not! That water is filled with gasoline and sewage and god knows what else."

He grinned and splashed her again.

This time she retaliated, dipping her paddle into the water and sending a cascading splash of water down his back.

Geoff's body recoiled. "Damn that's cold."

"Refreshing." Avery dissolved into giggles.

Her laughter eased the knot in Geoff's chest. Their whole first date had done more for his mood and his business stats than he'd ever imagined. Date two was not going to go down in flames because of some questionable press.

"I'm glad you're amused," he said.

"I am." Avery grinned at him and aimed another splash his way. Then she suddenly dropped the paddle into the water.

"What are you doing?" Geoff leaned over the side of his kayak to fish the paddle out of the water. "That's not part of the plan."

Avery's eyes were wide and surprised, and a blush stole across her face. "I may have just had a wardrobe malfunction."

He glanced at her life preserver. "You look okay to me."

"No, not the life vest." She shook her head and laughed. "Underneath. Pretty sure the clasp on my bathing suit just gave out."

What he wouldn't have given to have seen that without the life preserver on top. "Want me to see if I can fix it?" he asked.

Avery bit her lip. "Yeah."

Geoff drew his boat near hers once more and balanced both paddles across his kayak while she unclipped her life preserver.

"Here I go again, breaking the rules," she muttered. She slid the life vest off her shoulders and pressed one hand against her chest to hold her bathing suit in place. Then she twisted to the side so he could examine her back.

One prong on the bathing suit's plastic clasp had sheared off, leaving it useless. "Yep. Definitely busted." Geoff grinned. "What can I say, it just couldn't restrain your considerable…"

"Muscles!" she shrieked.

"That's what I was going to say."

She snorted. "Right. And don't you dare say I told you so about the suit."

Geoff bit back a smile. When he'd first seen her pull off her cover-up today to reveal the skimpy bikini, he'd told her, "You look great Cheese Girl. But is the suit functional?"

She'd shot him a look. "It functions to cover my body."

But, clearly, it wasn't designed to do anything more than look good. Geoff cleared his throat now. "All I was going to say is that I think I can tie the back instead."

"Sure," she said like she didn't believe him.

Geoff reached for the skinny straps that crisscrossed under Avery's shoulder blades and tied the ends together. As he did, his fingers brushed her sun-warmed skin, the tiny touch surprisingly sensual.

She stilled with a small gasp, and he paused, his fingers resting on her skin.

Oh god. This girl. What was she doing to him?

He sucked in a deep breath and pulled away.

Avery broke the silence. "What do you say we head back to the dock?" She glanced over her shoulder at him. "I'm ready for the next part of our lesson."

"What's that?"

She twisted her mouth and flicked her warm eyes back toward the shore. "I want you to teach me how to flirt."

"ARE you really sure you want to do this?"

Geoff eyed the guy behind the counter of the kayak rental stand and felt his shoulders stiffen. "Because if we're following the premise that you and I are dating, I can't imagine why I'd want to encourage you to flirt with someone else."

Avery laughed and zipped her hands over the bulky material of her life vest. "Are you jealous, Rock?"

He rubbed a hand over his jaw and answered honestly. "Yeah, maybe."

"Oh." Her eyes went wide, but she still shook her head. Her voice was tiny. "We're following the model where you tell me what I'm doing wrong and help me get better at this whole dating thing. So this lesson is about flirting."

"Ave, there is nothing wrong with the way you flirt. You just need to be yourself. Stop worrying what everyone else thinks."

"Right now it matters that the whole world thinks I'm not a credible spokesperson for X Enterprises. So it does matter that I can do this."

Geoff's eyebrows rose. "You're not credible because you said you hadn't been on three dates with the same person?"

She shrugged. "Yeah, that's part of it."

"Avery, anyone with two brain cells to rub together would know that your personal life and your ability to do your job are two different things."

She snorted out a laugh. "Yes, but in advertising, we're always playing to the lowest common denominator. The people who don't actually have the brain cells to rub together to make that connection."

"Okay, fine." He sighed. "Let's teach you how to flirt."

Avery clapped her hands together and grinned. "Thank you. Now point me in the right direction."

Geoff swept his eyes over her body. "For starters, the life jacket may have been necessary out on the water, but it's hiding your killer curves right now."

She bit her bottom lip and looked up at him with big eyes. "Killer curves? Man, you know how to sweet talk a girl."

He smiled at her, forcing his voice to stay light. "I'm an expert for a reason." He pointed at her ensemble. "Lose the jacket, Cheese."

She unbuckled it and slid the life jacket from her shoulders, revealing her tiny teal bathing suit. Avery's shoulders were pink from the afternoon on the water, and the faintest highlights streaked the strands of hair that fell from the bun on top of her head.

Geoff's throat grew thick, and he swallowed hard. "Good. Now let your hair down."

She looked up at him uncertainly. "I thought you said the packaging didn't matter."

"Someone who's worth hanging around with you is going to see past the packaging, yeah. But you're making a quick first impression here. It's better to stack the odds."

Avery loosened her hair from her bun, and it fell around her shoulders in soft, damp waves. She ran her hands through the strands, fanning them around her face. She looked like one of those beachy surfer girls in an advertisement for Hawaii, and he'd take that vacation any day.

"Now what?"

"Physical contact is good because it shows your interest. When you talk to him, go for little innocent touches here and there. A hand on the arm, whatever."

Avery nodded.

"And laugh a lot. Guys love to feel like we're hilarious."

She rolled her eyes. "I'll bet you do."

"No, hear me out. Our natural instinct is to want to impress you, and since most dudes are unlikely to flaunt their bankroll the first time you meet, an appreciation for their humor goes far."

Avery dropped her hands to her hips, accentuating her waist. Geoff forced his eyes away from her bellybutton and back to her face. She gave a half-twirl. "Am I ready, O Dating Guru?"

"Yeah, Cheese. You look good."

She gave him a satisfied smile and strode toward the rental counter. "Wish me luck."

The words stuck in his throat.

Geoff watched Avery's ass in her tiny bikini bottom, the sight a small consolation prize. She reached the counter and pointed toward their two kayaks. Then she leaned forward, touching the rental guy's forearm, and laughed.

This was a bad idea.

Geoff looked away, his hands fisting at his sides. Across the water, a few seagulls wheeled in the sunlight, calling to each other. He kept his gaze on them until Avery's footsteps shook the dock once more.

He turned to face her, and from her grin, he knew she'd done well.

"Got a number," she crowed. She nudged his shoulder with hers. "Told him you were my brother, and it was smooth sailing from there."

"Great," he ground out.

She sucked in a quick breath. "Are you mad at me?"

"Are you going to use that number?"

Avery's face transformed with uncertainty. "No, probably not."

He nodded. It did make him feel a little better, but he'd be damned if he told her that. He moved his gaze away from her face. It was easier not to look at her. "Ave, I was wrong about what's sexy, okay?"

"But I got a number."

"Any guy with two eyes to see is going to give you his number. Hell, a blind guy would give you his number just from the way your voice sounds like a girl in a beer commercial. And yeah, part of being sexy is the combination of all those things I just suggested. But it's more than that, too. Sexy is owning exactly who you are. The other stuff is surface, Avery. Your heart is sexy. Your laugh is sexy. You are sexy whether or not you try."

Her hand landed on his arm, and heat shot through him. "Sorry, Geoff. I was getting a little carried away there."

"It's okay." He shrugged it off. This was what they'd both signed up for.

"It's not." Her voice softened, vulnerable. "The date I want to be on is this one, in case I didn't make that clear."

Geoff turned and brought his eyes to hers. "Are you sure, Cheese Girl?"

She cracked a grin. "I'm sure, Rock."

"In that case, would you like to practice flirting with me back at my place?"

Her mouth dropped open. "Ummm..."

He laughed. "You're in a bathing suit, and I've got a hot tub." He started walking down the dock and felt a burst of pride as she hurried to follow him. "Take that as you will."

CHAPTER 9

*a*very settled against the wall of Geoff's hot tub and sighed. The hot tub was out on Geoff's balcony, overlooking Capitol Hill and downtown beyond that, and below her, the city teemed with people. It was sunset now, and the lights in all the buildings had started to show up against the darkening sky like sparkles.

"How did I not notice this the first time I was here?" she asked.

The jets sent a steady stream of warm water against her lower back and shoulders and brought a rush of bubbles to the surface of the hot tub. She could feel her face flush from the heat, and she let her muscles relax. With the flirting experiment successfully conducted, she'd pulled her hair back into a bun, and now the water tugged a few errant strands loose from the grip of her ponytail holder.

"You were too busy talking about sex toys." Geoff's grin reached into her stomach and made it flutter.

She tilted her head and smiled at him. "Must be." She had to raise her voice above the noise of the jets, and rumbling of the motor spread into her chest.

Avery closed her eyes and opened them to find Geoff's gaze on her face, his expression serious.

"What's wrong?" she asked.

"You look beautiful."

The timed jets cut out at that moment, leaving the word "beautiful" dangling in the air, loud in the sudden silence.

Oh.

Avery's chest heated, and she swirled a hand through the water. "You know, when I was a little girl, I always wanted my own hot tub."

"You did?"

She nodded. "It seemed like the height of sophistication and glamour. Like if I was sitting in a hot tub, just chilling out, I would have made it."

Geoff smiled at her. "And here you are. Fancy PR job at a sexy company, the world at your feet. Rocking everything you do."

Avery laughed. "Not quite. I just wanted to show everyone that I could be like one of those people in the magazines. I didn't have a lot of money growing up, so it felt really important to me to be able to fit in, be comfortable. I know now it's all Photoshop, so whatever."

Geoff leaned against his side of the hot tub, and his knee drifted into hers, solid and strong. The muscles of his chest stretched wide and tempting. What would it be like to touch him there, to put her hand on his heart once more?

"I didn't know you guys weren't well off," he said.

She shrugged like it didn't matter, but it had. At least back then. "By the time I met you, my parents were doing fine. But my dad spent a lot of my childhood in and out of work." Avery frowned. "Mostly out. We were happy, you know, but in the way that little kids can be when they don't know any better. But over time, I started to notice all the places where my life didn't line up with my friends'. Like how we'd always do birthdays in the backyard with just a friend or two instead of a whole class party, and how my mom always packed my lunch and said it was healthier that way.

"One time I begged for lunch money on pizza day, because it was my favorite. And we didn't have money enough for that, so she sent me with English muffin pizzas made with canned pasta sauce so she could also use the sauce for pasta."

Geoff nudged her. "If it helps, you are totally the height of glamour."

She shook her head but smiled. "You were right, you know."

Geoff stood, and rivulets of water sluiced over his skin as he reached for the button on the hot tub to kick the jets back on. This time when he sat, he moved his body closer to hers. Hip to hip, shoulder to shoulder.

The jets started up again with a groan.

Avery bit her lip and looked away, out over the city. The sun was dipping over the horizon line, tinting the sky the palest pink. Now that fall was here, night came earlier, and the sunburn on her shoulders was the only hint that the day had been warm enough for swimsuits.

"I was right about what?" Geoff asked.

"The things that make me feel good aren't surface things or the glamorous things. They're laughing really deeply, the feeling of sun on my face. The way my muscles right now are so tired from kayaking that I'm just loose and happy." She dropped her eyes. "Sorry, cheesy confession."

"It's not cheesy, Cheese Girl."

She groaned.

"Just so you know, when you let yourself be happy, that's incredibly sexy." Geoff's voice was rough and deep.

"Oh yeah?"

His throaty reply sounded like a confession. "Yeah." He hesitated before continuing. "Ave, something's changed. That kiss, it was..."

Real? Fake? Her chest tightened. She hated that it mattered so much to her when it seemed to be something he was going to use to his advantage.

She interrupted before Geoff could continue, trying to make this fit into whatever fake-dating plan they'd concocted. It was easier that way. "That's what you would do, right? If you liked someone?"

He cleared his throat. "Yeah."

"So then it's fine." She made her voice go light and perky. "You're not crossing any lines."

But it was a lie. The boundaries had blurred so she didn't know which way was up anymore. If she was fake-dating him, was she allowed to develop real feelings? Could she let her body act knowing nothing was for real?

Geoff nudged her foot with his. "Is it okay that I want to do that again?"

Avery's lips curved into a smile, and she let herself give the answer that

57

felt the most true. "It's more than okay," she whispered. But she didn't expect the way her stomach flipped and her heart kicked up in her chest. Was he acting the part or did he really mean it?

"Good," Geoff murmured, turning to her. He leaned one hand across her body to steady himself against the hot tub wall and brought the other hand to her jaw. He smelled like chlorine and soap, like sunlight. She leaned into his touch, and her eyes fluttered closed.

Geoff's lips grazed hers, gently, like an exploration.

His kiss was a call in the dark.

Avery answered in kind, her nose against his, her body softening against every hard plane of his chest. His fingers tightened in her hair, pulling her close, and the deep, lush kiss intensified with every breath.

Geoff groaned and leaned back, breathing heavy. "God, Avery." His dark eyes on hers sent a rush of blood to her head and straight down between her thighs.

He adjusted his body and reached for her, pulling her through the water so her body felt weightless and floating. She collided with his chest, and he dragged her down on his lap, the thin material of his bathing suit straining over an impressive erection.

Well. He probably wasn't faking that.

Avery held one hand against the delicious, toned muscle of his shoulder and placed a knee on the bench on either side of him. From her position on top, she could rock into him, and the friction of his body against hers sent sparks over her skin.

She might be soaring.

She might never hit the ground again.

Avery brought her mouth to his, controlling the kiss, not caring or wondering or asking if this was real. She let herself live in the moment, taking from it, and her whole body lit on fire.

Geoff's chest rumbled against hers, and the pressure from the water jets batted against his back and streamed through his arms to push against her chest. Her pulse was in her ears, and everything fell away. This felt like the stadium kiss, but better.

Deeper.

More.

Geoff traced a hand down her spine to cup her ass, lowered his mouth to a spot below her ear and brought a rush of warmth to her skin. His mouth explored her neck at the same time his fingers explored her under the water, trailing over her hip to dip between their bodies.

Avery let out a moan as he found a sensitive spot on her hip that made her squirm.

"You like that?" She could feel his grin against her neck.

"I do."

Geoff bit her gently, then swirled his tongue over her skin to soothe it. Then he reached a finger under the edge of her bikini bottom, and she stiffened.

"Wait." Avery broke the kiss, and heat rushed to her face. Geoff searched her eyes, a frown on his gorgeous lips, and she dropped her gaze. "There's something you should know. In the name of authenticity."

"Nothing you say is going to scare me away."

Doubtful.

Avery swallowed hard. "I haven't done this before."

"Made out in a hot tub?" Geoff glanced over her shoulder. "We can totally go inside if you want."

"No, Geoff. I haven't had sex before."

Geoff's eyebrows rose, and his mouth did a funny thing, twisting to the side in a question.

Well, shit.

Her heart dropped as she pushed away from him. "That's it, isn't it? When I say I'm a virgin, it destroys everything." Her chest tightened, and she sank onto the bench across from him, out of reach. This is what always happened to her, the reason sex had become this huge thing in her head. She just wanted to get it over with already. But it wasn't fair to hold back that information from a guy, either. Not when she was ready to take that next step.

And with Geoff, she was.

Avery's voice wobbled. "I'm either too inexperienced to train, or I become some conquest."

She watched Geoff's throat dip as he swallowed. "Avery, it's okay. I told you before you're not a conquest for me. Why don't we take the idea of sex off the table?"

Oh.

He didn't want to have sex with her.

Dammit.

Avery blinked back at him, stung. Guess this was another signal she'd read wrong. This was just a make-out session for the sake of making out. Nothing more. No real attraction. No possibility of sex. Just the game, rearing its ugly head.

The rejection felt like a slap.

"Right," she said, forcing herself to shrug. "Sure."

She'd just ruined everything. Or he had. It was hard to say.

The timer on the water jets kicked off, plunging them into silence.

CHAPTER 10

"*A*nd that concludes this week's episode of *How to Hook a Hottie*. Check in next week for my third and final date with Avery. Will we or won't we keep seeing each other? Until next time, here's a final word from our sponsors."

Geoff cut in the sponsor message and then faded out the show.

Well, damn.

That was a train wreck.

It had become uncomfortable to tell a group of strangers how it had felt to kiss Avery, how it had felt when her soft body landed on top of his in the hot tub, with the water swirling all around them and everything this slippery heat. He'd resorted to being vague and non-specific, and the storyteller inside of him cringed. It didn't help that he'd live-streamed the show, and anyone who watched could see his face twitch as he struggled with what to say. The video component of *How to Hook a Hottie* had always set him apart in a good way, but no longer.

Geoff opened the chat window that had appeared during the livestream and skimmed through the comments.

Where are the details? gym4lifetho complained. *Missing out on the hot stuff.*

Love hearing about you and Avery! You sound so happy! Mel0801 chimed in.

So, great. Which was it?

Geoff rubbed a hand over his hair and rolled his desk chair away from the computer. He reached for the phone and texted Ryan, his friend from high school who made a living these days as a graphic designer building websites for small businesses and bored stay-at-home moms.

I need a break, Geoff texted. *Want to hit the gym?*

Let me wrap up this email, Ryan replied. *Be there in fifteen minutes.*

Good.

Geoff padded to the bedroom and slipped into his gym clothes before striding toward the front door. On the walk through his apartment, his eyes slid over to the hot tub and paused there. His chest tightened, and he forced himself to walk through the front door.

It wasn't just that Avery was a record and he kept playing her music. It was that he was fucking stuck on the same track, the memory of that night looping through his head over and over again.

Time to find a new song.

* * *

GEOFF RACKED up the weights on the leg press machine at Amped Fitness and adjusted the seat to the perfect angle. Then he flopped onto the chair, lining up his feet and straightening his legs to lift the weight.

One rep. Two.

"Have you ever had a girl go hot and cold on you?" he asked.

Ryan squirted an electrolyte drink into his mouth and swirled it around before swallowing it. He narrowed his eyes at Geoff. "Aren't you the dating expert?"

Geoff pressed out another few reps, grateful that the strain on his quads gave him something to concentrate on.

"I mean, yeah, but this hasn't quite happened before. If a girl's into me, I usually know it. I can't get a handle on this one."

"Who is she?"

Another rep, the sweat popping out on his forehead. "Have you been listening to the show?"

Ryan shot him an unabashed grin. "Why should I listen to your show? Literally tens of thousands of people tell you how great you are, and you pretty much give me the play by play after you record anyway." He aimed another squirt of liquid into his mouth and started to swish.

Geoff rolled his eyes but nodded. "Fair point. It's Avery Beeker."

Ryan coughed, and water sprayed from his mouth. "Avery Beeker? From high school? Your little sister's best friend?" Ryan started mopping up the liquid with a threadbare gym towel. "I didn't know that was a thing."

Geoff grimaced and straightened his legs for his final rep. "Yeah, well, she's not so little anymore. She's the PR person for X Enterprises. Let's just say she embodies the role." The leg press machine clanged as he let the weights drop. Up at the front of the gym, a bored employee shot him a look of annoyance.

Whatever.

Geoff stood and wiped off his seat, letting Ryan take his place. "Anyway, we're doing a segment for the show. A three-date setup to help her get better at dating."

Ryan re-racked the weights and started his set. "So these dates—are they real or not?"

Geoff let out a puff of air. "I don't actually know the answer to that question. They feel kind of real. And I mean, the way she kissed me felt real. But she also jumped out of my hot tub the other day like she found out it was infected with dysentery or E. coli or something. She made a sorry excuse for having to work and then bailed."

Ryan grinned. "Sonofabitch. Sounds like you need to figure some stuff out." Geoff nodded, and Ryan continued. "And the dates are just to teach her?"

Geoff's fingers twitched. Teach her. Avery the virgin. Avery the virgin who made a living writing dirty descriptions for sex toys. Avery who was innocent but not.

How was he supposed to wrap his mind around that one?

And why was the idea of being the one to deflower her so damn tempting?

Ryan relinquished the seat, and Geoff sat back down to start a fresh round of reps. "Yeah," Geoff said. "But the idea of her using those skills with anyone else doesn't feel great."

Ryan grunted. "How many dates has it been now?"

"Two." Geoff's muscles strained as he lifted the weights.

Ryan rubbed his hands together. "So you've got a big date coming up then."

Geoff paused, his legs and lungs burning. "Number three."

"What do you want to come out of this?" Ryan rubbed his chin. "You going to close the deal?"

Geoff groaned and pressed out another rep. "I don't actually know. I like her. My sister likes her. My audience is split."

"Your audience?"

"It matters." It shouldn't matter, but it did. That was the reality of his life. Geoff gritted his teeth. "I have sponsors to report to and stats that I need to maintain. My show is built on the principle of me trying out dating techniques in the field. Where would things even go from here?"

"Wait a second," Ryan said. "Weren't you dating some girl a few years back? That was fine, right?"

"I dated her for three weeks."

"See, there you go."

"No." Geoff shook his head. "I dated her for three weeks, and my ratings plummeted. My fans kept saying I was a sellout, like finding someone to hang out with consistently was against the single-guy code."

Ryan made a face. "Rough."

"Yeah. The relationship would have crashed anyway, but it didn't leave a good taste in my mouth. And even if things were going to work out with Avery, I can't help wondering if it would be a good thing or if it would just tank my show."

"Okay, well forget everyone else for a minute. Do you want to date her?"

Geoff paused. His heart screamed *yes*, and his head told him to slow the fuck down. "I don't know," he said at last. "But I want to see where this goes."

Ryan nodded. "Then it sounds pretty simple to me. You either want to date her or not. And if you want her, you need to show her that."

"Right," Geoff said, but it wasn't simple at all. His muscles gave out, and he let the weights drop.

CHAPTER 11

*W*ould Geoff like her hair up or down? Avery studied herself in the mirror, piling her hair on top of her head. With it out of her face, her cheekbones definitely stood out, but when it was down, she looked more carefree. And for Geoff, who seemed to think she was trying too hard, maybe that was better.

She let out a puff of air and dropped her hair.

Who the hell cared?

This was the highest number of consecutive dates she'd been on with anyone in the last year, but it wasn't even for real. She was only still going because she needed to fix her credibility issue.

And because maybe she'd take another kiss from Geoff, even if it was under false pretenses. Kissing him was fun, whether or not it was real.

The doorbell rang, and Avery's stomach tensed. Geoff was early.

She strode through her apartment, calling out as she approached the front door. "Where does appearing overeager fit into your three-act structure?"

She swung open the door and gasped.

"I have no idea what you're talking about." Sophie stood in her doorway clutching a bottle of rosé and a RiteAid shopping bag. A gossip magazine poked out of the top of the bag, and something inside clanked as she walked into Avery's apartment. Nail polish, probably.

"Sophie, hi." Avery's cheeks burned, and she glanced at her watch. Ten minutes to get rid of her. "Sorry, thought you were someone else."

Sophie raised an eyebrow. "Who?"

"Um, just a neighbor. A playwright. We've been having debates about… plays…in the laundry room."

Sophie's forehead furrowed while she tried to puzzle that one out. Then she shrugged and pressed the bottle of wine into Avery's hands.

"Ready for a girls' night?"

Avery frowned. "I'd love to, Soph, but I've got plans tonight."

"Oh." Sophie's face fell. "It's just you've been busy the last few weekends, and I miss you."

"I'm swamped with this huge project for work." At least it was sort of true.

"Bummer." Sophie tried to soften her words with a smile. "But I'm glad you're so ambitious."

"Thank you."

Her friend glanced over Avery's shoulder. "So, you don't happen to have some secret lover stashed in your closet right now, do you?"

"What?" Avery sputtered. She almost lost her grip on the wine, and she scrambled to tighten her grasp on the slick bottle. "No. Definitely not."

Sophie frowned like she didn't quite believe her. "That's an awfully sexy dress."

There was no way she knew, was there? Avery cocked her head to the side. "Have you been listening to Geoff's show?"

Sophie shook her head. "I told you, I don't pay attention to my brother's dating show. It's a conflict of interest. And really, I don't need any more evidence that he's a pig."

"He's not that bad," Avery muttered, but her shoulders relaxed ever so slightly.

Sophie barged on. "He is. And those girls who actually fall for his crap? How can I respect them when they don't even respect themselves?"

Ouch.

Avery rubbed the heel of her hand over her chest. She'd started to fall for it, hadn't she? It's why this was all so damn confusing.

"What time are your plans?" Sophie asked. "Do you at least have time for a quick drink?"

"Um, actually, I'm heading out in a second. Just need to put on my shoes."

Sophie's face pinched, and Avery's stomach squeezed. "Tell you what," Avery said. "I do have a way we might get to see each other a bit more. Jeremy and Vanessa at my work are trying to figure out wedding favors, and when I was brainstorming to help them, I suggested cookies. Nothing sexy, just totally on brand. If I could get you the gig baking them, would you want it?"

Sophie's face shone. "What? Seriously?"

Avery nodded.

"That's only the biggest wedding on the social calendar." Sophie's eyes sparkled. "The kind of event that could boost my business even more."

"Yep." Avery smiled. If anyone deserved a chance to get in front of some big players, it was Sophie.

Sophie squealed and threw her arms around Avery's neck. "Yes! Thank you."

"Of course. Now get out of here so I can finish getting ready."

Sophie turned on her heel and marched back toward the front door. "Keep the wine for next time."

Avery clutched the bottle to her chest. "You bet." She walked into the kitchen to put away the bottle as Sophie let herself out.

"What the hell?" Sophie's shocked tone made a spike of panic stick in Avery's throat.

Oh shit.

It couldn't be Geoff. She still had a good five minutes, and what guy showed up to a date early?

"Nice to see you too, squirt."

Avery's whole body cringed. Teeth to stomach to face. Parts of her body she didn't even know could cringe cringed.

Oh, holy shit.

She sucked in a deep breath and turned.

Geoff stood in Avery's front entry wearing dress pants and a white button-down shirt, throwing off sexy bachelor boss vibes. Something about the contrast between his crisp, white shirt and his dark hair and five o'clock shadow made her heart thump. Beside him, Sophie's red face and raised shoulders betrayed how very pissed she was.

"This isn't what it looks like!" Avery yelped, hurrying toward the door.

Geoff shut the door behind him and leaned his hip against the wall, a cocky grin on his face.

Sophie gave Avery an accusing glare. "It looks like my brother just showed up at your house in date night clothes."

"Geoff and I have a business arrangement." Avery smiled, trying to force it to be true. But her heart still leaped at the sight of him, her core tightening for him. "We're heading to dinner to discuss how he's going to share the news with his audience that I am not, in fact, hopeless at dating, and that I'm a total industry expert."

Sophie's shoulders lowered a tiny bit, but her face remained skeptical. "I take it the first show didn't go as planned?"

Avery's cheeks heated. "Not exactly."

"And this is just business?" Sophie looked between the two of them like she was trying to sniff out a lie. "Because it looks awfully fancy for a business dinner on a Saturday night."

Geoff cleared his throat. "You know me—if I go out, I do it in style."

"Not a date," Avery confirmed.

"Good. Because I'm not about to let my older brother come between us. And since dating him has led to disaster for every other female on the planet so far, it could be the kind of thing that could change everything."

A breath puffed out of her. "Why?"

"Because I don't want to clean up his mess. Because I don't want to have to split my loyalty between him and you. I love you both."

Geoff rubbed a thumb over his lower lip. "You know, even if something happened between me and Cheese Girl, I'm sure your friendship is strong enough to overcome anything."

Sophie shrugged. "That may be true, but I'm still shutting down that possibility. Common sense rules in my favor."

Avery's throat felt tight. Sophie had always been a voice of reason for her, but this was one piece of advice she had a hard time wanting to follow. Even though she should.

* * *

GEOFF SWALLOWED the last dregs of his wine and smiled at Avery. "That was delicious."

"It was." Her own plate had been scraped clean, Osteria La Spiga's tagliatelle with white truffle butter devoured within minutes. A candle flickered on the wood-topped table between them, and the sound of happy patrons and tinkling silverware filled the restaurant.

"Are you ready for dessert?" Geoff's voice was a low promise, a smooth seduction.

Avery ran her fingers over the napkin in her lap. "First the cookie, now this. You're always trying to make me break my diet."

He cocked an eyebrow but responded without heat. "As a pointer, don't talk about your diet. You're at the stage of dating where everything needs to feel like a possibility, including dessert."

She swallowed hard. "Including sex?"

"Yeah." He licked his lips. "Including sex." His eyes were dark and so deeply sensual that she was about ready to hand over her V-card to him, propriety be damned.

"But you took it off the table," she whispered. She needed to say it out loud to remind herself. Geoffrey Carter did not want to have sex with her.

Crap.

Geoff groaned. "That's not the point."

Wasn't it, though?

He leaned forward, resting his elbows on the table and folding his hands under his chin. "Live a little, Cheese Girl. If I recall, you had a very positive response to sugar the other day. I'd like to see you that happy again."

71

Avery blushed. "Okay, fine. Let's go get dessert." She pointed a finger at him. "But only if you promise to make me look good on your show."

Geoff grinned at her teasing tone, his eyes catching the candlelight from their table. "Deal. But you really don't need to be so worried about what everyone else thinks." He stood and offered her his hand. "And anyway, you already look good." He grazed his eyes over her dress, and she sucked in a breath.

"I meant for your audience."

He tipped his head at her. "The vast majority of my audience loves you."

"The vast majority?" She slid her hand into his and frowned at him. "I didn't know this was a statistics lesson."

He squeezed her hand and laughed. "The ones who love you are going to be true fans." He led her toward the restaurant's front door. "As for the rest, who cares? You're not going to impress everyone."

Avery frowned. "Well when it comes to dating, isn't that the point?"

Geoff shook his head, his voice serious. "No." He placed a hand on her lower back and guided her through the front door and onto the street.

His touch, burning through the thin fabric of her dress, also burned away her senses. It took her a second to regain her voice. "In PR, we're trying to reach the widest range of our target customers. So I thought impressing more people would be good."

They turned left, walking around the corner shoulder to shoulder. "Right, but they're still your target customers," Geoff said. "Let's face it, Ave, you're not out to land the ex-frat boy who doesn't care that you prefer strawberry ice cream to vanilla and who doesn't care that you like soccer and that you played center striker in eleventh grade."

He'd paid attention. He didn't just know her favorite ice cream flavor—he'd remembered the damn position she'd played ten years ago.

Still, Avery stiffened at the frat boy line, unable to hide the way it hit too close to home.

"This okay?" Geoff asked, and she was about to respond that she could land whoever she wanted when she realized he'd stopped short in front of Cupcake Royale.

He'd meant *was the cupcake store okay*. Not *was his comment okay*.

Right.

"Yeah, it's perfect."

Geoff held open the door for her, and the scent of butter and sugar and ice cream wafted through the air. Avery crossed the threshold and paused, closing her eyes and breathing in a deep gulp of air. The smells washed over her body, relaxing her and making her smile.

She opened her eyes and caught Geoff staring at her. Her skin tingled. "What? Do I have something in my teeth?"

"No, Ave." He curled one hand around hers, then leaned forward so his mouth was against her ear, all radiating heat and promise. Was it bad that she wanted to lean into him? To feel his mouth on her neck once more? "That was the sexiest breath of air I think I've ever witnessed."

Her lips tugged into a smile. If he was going to play this game, then so was she. "Now imagine if I was coming instead of just smelling cupcakes," she whispered back.

Geoff's fingers tightened around her hand. "Jesus Christ."

"See, I'm not so terrible at the flirting thing."

"Never said you were. I think that was all in your head. You know exactly how to get a guy's attention."

Her satisfied smile stretched wider. "Just because I haven't...you know...doesn't mean I'm not a fan."

Geoff shot her a dark look. "You don't need to prove yourself to me."

Her cheeks heated. "I know," she said quietly.

Open mouth. Insert foot.

Geoff turned his attention to the cupcake display. "What's it going to be tonight, Ave?"

Wasn't that the question?

She stepped forward and peered through the glass, where buttercream frosting swirled temptingly on top of huge cupcakes.

"I can't decide between a red velvet and a Dance Party," she said.

He grinned. "One of each," he told the employee behind the display case.

Geoff paid for the cupcakes and led Avery to a cozy corner booth in the store.

They sat to eat, splitting the two cupcakes so a sugar buzz made her chest soar. He smiled at her, attentive, his eyes on her face as they chatted, and it would be so easy to let this flirtation keep going. First the fancy dinner, now this. Geoff had gone above and beyond to make tonight really special for her, and he looked so good in his pressed shirt—smelled so good. It would be so easy to give in to him. To let herself get carried away like she had the other day in the hot tub.

Avery finished the last bite of her vanilla-vanilla cupcake and licked her lips, fiddling with the empty cupcake wrapper on her plate.

"You look like you're deciding if you want another one," Geoff laughed.

She shook her head.

"Solving world peace, then?"

"Trying to decide how this all fits into your three-date structure." She cringed at her own honesty.

Hesitation flashed on Geoff's face, and he twisted his mouth.

There.

She knew she'd just gotten swept up in his charm. Dating girls was what he was so good at doing—hell, he'd made a career doing it. But he was a player, and if she wasn't careful, she was going to get played.

Tonight wasn't real, even if she wanted it to be.

"Avery, you're different than any other girl I've met." Geoff's voice was quiet. "You're smart and funny and kind."

She frowned and dropped her eyes. "That may be true. But you didn't say sexy."

"Sexy, Ave. Sexy as hell. I thought that was pretty fucking clear." The sincerity in his tone made her glance up, and she found his eyes dark and sensual. The heat in his gaze set her core on fire, and everything in her body tightened in anticipation.

"So have I learned all my lessons?" she asked, trying to keep her voice steady.

"I guess it depends what you want to know." Geoff's words were a low invitation.

What would it be like to take the next step with him? Would it matter if it wasn't for real? Her body wanted it, that was for sure.

Avery bit her lip and stared into his gorgeous eyes, longing and logic warring inside her. She drew a deep breath and opened her mouth. "Geoff, is there any chance you could take me home?"

CHAPTER 12

*G*eoff parked his car on the curb outside of Avery's apartment and cut the engine. With the air conditioning in the car turned off, the windows fogged ever so slightly with the heat of him and the gorgeous girl next to him. He leaned his arm on the backrest of her seat, his heart pounding.

"Home sweet home."

Avery glanced out the window and rubbed a hand over her arm. "Thank you."

She'd said she wanted him to bring her home, and from the look on her face in Cupcake Royale, he'd have been willing to bet she wanted to kiss him. So why wasn't she inviting him in?

Geoff wanted to explore her apartment, see the spot she ate breakfast every morning, maybe even see her bed. He wouldn't push the sex thing, obviously. She wasn't ready, or maybe he wasn't. But having her moan into his mouth the way she'd done the other night? His cock twitched at just the thought.

Avery wasn't saying anything, so he spoke instead. "When can I take you out next?"

Her eyes widened. "Go out again? Like a date?"

"Yeah, Cheese Girl. I like being around you."

"Oh." Her voice trembled before the silence of the car swallowed it. "But the show's over, right? Three episodes for three dates?"

"Who cares?"

Her face crumpled, and she darted her eyes away. A muscle in her face tightened, and a crease formed between her eyebrows. "I think we should just be friends." She said it with great effort, like it hurt, and dammit, it did.

Geoff blinked at her, unable to process how fast things had changed. "Are you serious?"

She still wouldn't meet his eye. "Yeah. It'll be easier. With Sophie, and all."

"I'm sorry, you're using Sophie as an excuse?" He shouldn't want to kiss Avery this badly. He shouldn't want to wrap his arms around her and sink into her. It could destroy everything—his reputation, his career, his relationship with his sister. As much as he wanted to argue her last point, Avery wasn't entirely wrong.

She sighed. "You heard how much she's against this. And maybe she's right. Don't take this the wrong way, but you're not exactly long-term material yourself."

"What?" In the three years he'd been running *How to Hook a Hottie*, he'd only ever been told he was a catch. He was driven and successful, made more than enough money, and had taken enough press photos to know he cleaned up well. And, yeah, he hadn't been in any long-term relationships, but that was kind of required by the show.

He sat back, stung, and his voice came out flinty and hard. "Another pointer, Ave. If you want to get anywhere, don't cut a guy off at the knees."

Her bitter laugh was a knife. "I'm sure you can handle it."

Where had he gone wrong? In the store, she'd implied he should hear her orgasm, and now she was tearing down everything he'd built, her words crushing like a sledgehammer through drywall.

Geoff yanked his arm from the back of her seat and raked a hand through his hair. "I don't think you're being fair right now. I like you. You like me."

"The point is, whatever I do want, Geoff, it's something real. Not something staged for your show. And I don't even know what this is."

"Me neither. But I'm willing to find out."

But instead of agreeing, she slung her purse over her shoulder and reached for the door handle. "Thanks again for a great night, Geoff. I really enjoyed myself." Her words were flat, like she was only saying the lines to be nice. She was putting all those uptight rules into place again, washing away the looser, carefree girl he'd started to crave.

"Sure." He nodded, her words not quite sinking in.

Avery opened the car door and walked toward her home with her spine straight. Geoff sat there, stunned, as he let her slip away.

GEOFF LOOKED through his studio window out at the sprawl of Seattle. The trees on the street below had started dropping leaves, and on this morning's run through the city, he'd finally needed to trade in his T-shirt for a long-sleeved running shirt. Inside his apartment, he'd kicked on the heat, and it chugged quietly in the background as he sat at his desk.

The day dripped rainy, and the light spilling onto his face through the window was like a weak tea. Still, he smiled for the rolling webcam.

"As far as things go, I'm going to chalk this up to being a super successful dating experiment. After the three dates with Avery, I think we both had a great feel for our initial chemistry."

High and sparking.

"Through our more active date, we were able to assess our ability to get through problems together."

Not at all. Not when she gave up on him without trying. It still stung, even four days later.

"And we were able to reach a final consensus as to whether or not we'd like to continue seeing each other."

Yes. No. Who the fuck knows?

"Since this experiment was done for the show, Avery and I are going to continue on as friends, the same way we started. I've got a show to run; she's got sex toys to sell."

His eyes snagged on the extra set of headphones, the one she'd worn during her time on the show a few short weeks ago. A strand of her hair was wrapped around the headphones, but she was gone. It hurt more than felt reasonable. Geoff took a deep breath, trying to loosen the knot in his chest.

"As you know, this dating experiment that Avery proposed was designed to see where she went wrong in the dating world. The truth is at the end of the day she didn't need my help at all. We did discover that the same principles I've applied to helping guys convert more dates into long-term relationships work when you flip them for women. When you're your authentic self, you'll increase the odds of having solid, lasting relationships.

"We're going to take a programming break for a few weeks, and when we return, I'll be diving into more dating tips and tricks and new interviews with industry experts. The show will go on. After all, there are many more lessons to share from the field."

He had to make it sound like this was his plan all along. Not like he'd been blindsided by a girl he'd known for years.

"So for now, follow along with my adventures on Instagram, Snapchat, and Twitter, and stay tuned when we return with the next season of the show."

Geoff rolled the sponsorship message and faded out the audio.

He needed to get his ass in gear and figure out where the hell he went from here. But first, he needed a drink.

CHAPTER 13

"*H*ey, Ave. Did you get a chance to listen to *How to Hook a Hottie* yesterday?"

Avery tore her eyes away from her computer monitor and caught Vanessa's eye. "Nope. I haven't listened to any of the dating recap episodes."

Vanessa nodded, her face compassionate. "I can imagine it would be weird to hear someone else talk about you to tens of thousands of people."

Avery sputtered out a laugh. "To put it lightly." She didn't want to know what Geoff thought about her. Only she did.

Still, no matter how tempting it would have been to tune in, it was safer this way. She couldn't trust her own emotions, let alone trust something he'd say for the show. And she'd made her decision. He didn't want her, and she needed to stay away. It was the right thing to do, even if it sucked.

Vanessa tilted her head, her dark hair cascading down her back. "You okay?"

Avery straightened her spine. "Yeah. Totally."

"If it helps, he had only good things to say about you and the company." Vanessa lowered her voice. "Between you and me, with the whole flower thing and the way he talks about you, I thought for sure you'd continue on to date four."

Dammit. This was the problem with letting people in, with peeling back the carefully constructed exterior she'd built her whole life. It was easier to hide behind the image of a girl who had it under control than to expose the parts of her that so desperately wanted approval. Because when it was her real self being judged, it hurt that much more.

Avery needed to get this conversation back on track, and even if she wasn't looking her best, she could still help Sophie. Sophie who she should have listened to all along.

"It was a PR thing," Avery reminded Vanessa. Even if it didn't feel that way. "And speaking of which, I know we talked about wedding favors the other day. Have you given more consideration to the idea of custom cookies? I was thinking you could frost your wedding logo on some cookies and have them hand-packaged for your guests."

Vanessa grinned. "It sounds delicious."

Avery smiled back. "Glad you think so. I actually have someone I'd like to recommend to you."

"A baker?"

"Yeah." Avery reached for her phone. "Let me show you her Instagram account." Vanessa smiled, and Avery tapped on the screen. Hundreds of food photos came up on Sophie's profile, arranged in a neat little grid. "You're going to love her."

* * *

"Knock, knock," Avery shouted, standing outside of Sophie's apartment door. She didn't have enough hands to actually knock, so this would have to do.

The sound of the TV from inside the apartment cut out, and as she shifted the two huge paper grocery bags on her hips, she could hear Sophie moving closer. Her friend swung open the door, and Avery grinned.

"Hello, gorgeous Insta-famous food blogger and now custom cookie decorator to the sex toy industry darlings."

Sophie's mouth dropped open. "Does that mean I got the gig?"

"That means you got the gig."

Sophie squealed and threw her arms around Avery's neck. "I'm surprised you had enough breath in your body to actually say all those words."

"I am feeling a little purple in the face," Avery managed. "How do I look?"

Sophie eyed the grocery bags. "You look like you could use a hand."

"Amen."

Sophie grabbed one of the bags from her and grunted at its weight. "Oof," she said, leading Avery inside. "What do you have in here?"

Avery grinned. "Literal pounds of butter. I was thinking we should get started with a few cookie samples. Really nail down your recipes and work on the design. There are only a few weeks until the wedding."

Maybe she could spend all of them here, baking and ignoring the way her stomach was tied up in knots over leaving Geoff alone in his car. The look of disappointment on his face was still burned into her mind. She'd thought she had made the right choice, only now her body ached like she'd run a half-marathon. It had to be her sex-deprived hormones messing with her because there was no way she was actually falling for him. Right?

"You had me at pounds of butter." Sophie dropped her bag onto the kitchen counter, and Avery followed suit. Sophie rubbed her hands together, then spun the dial on the oven to preheat it. "Maybe a simple sugar cookie to start? Those frost really well."

"I'm game. Tell me what you need me to do."

Sophie grinned. "Why don't you start by creaming together some butter and sugar?"

Avery snorted out a laugh as she washed her hands at the kitchen sink. "I know it's not supposed to sound so dirty, but every time I hear the word 'cream,' my mind wanders to some very inappropriate places."

"Why do you think bakers are always so happy?" Sophie asked. "Cream everywhere."

Avery threw a hand towel at Sophie, then burst into laughter. "I think I need more cream in my life. Sign me up."

Sophie caught the towel and bumped Avery's hip with her own. "Any prospects on that front? What about your playwright neighbor?"

Avery shook her head so violently she could add whiplash to her list of personal injuries.

Injured neck.

Injured heart.

"Nope. No. No, uh, creamy, prospects." She laughed awkwardly. "God, I've gotta stop saying that. Anyway, I've been keeping my head down at work, and that's my focus right now."

"Aww, come on." Sophie moved to the sink and began washing her hands. "There have to at least be some sexy coworkers at X Enterprises."

None who made her body radiate with need the way Geoffrey Carter did. Not that Sophie could ever know how Avery felt. Her friend had made it abundantly clear that her brother was off-limits, and that wasn't a line she wanted to cross right now. Especially since Geoff himself didn't seem to want to play the game.

"Sure," she agreed. "But I don't know the official company policy on dating your coworker."

"I mean, it worked for Jeremy and Vanessa, didn't it?"

Avery had to give her that one. "True. But I feel like you can get away with a lot more when you're the boss."

"Hmmm." Sophie shut off the water and dried her hands. "Well, keep me posted." She hung the towel over the bar on the oven door. "Fresh gossip or not, I'm glad you came over."

"This was way overdue," Avery agreed. She reached for a stick of butter and peeled back the edge of the wrapper.

"Plus, the fact that you ditched me for my brother? Ouch."

Avery's face heated. "I told you, it was a work thing." If she could say it enough times, it might start to be true. But the lie tasted bitter in her mouth, and she couldn't meet Sophie's eye. She dropped the butter into a mixing bowl and tossed the wrapper into the trash.

Sophie cocked her head. "Did you ever get him to do what you wanted?"

Avery froze near the trashcan. "What I wanted?" He'd kissed her, so that counted. But then he'd made it clear it was for the show. So that part had been a fail.

"On the show, or whatever." Sophie's clarification made Avery relax.

"Oh." Avery cleared her throat and hurried back to her bowl of butter. "Yeah, I guess. Vanessa at work seemed happy, so I think we're covered."

"That's good."

Sophie measured out some sugar and added it to Avery's bowl. The glittery white crystals shimmered like snowdrifts, and Avery wondered idly if they'd get snow in Seattle this year. The weather was changing, and the sun that had stretched into September had been replaced by an endless string of gray days.

"I kind of wish Geoff didn't have the show to begin with, you know?" Sophie said.

"What do you mean?"

Sophie sighed as she attached a pair of beaters to a handheld mixer. "Sometimes I wonder where Geoff's going to go from here. I hate listening to his show because I hate hearing him try to game people's hearts."

"To hear him say it, he's trying to help people find connections."

Sophie waved a free hand. "I know that's what he says. And clearly, he has enough listeners that people believe in his theories. But putting that aside, I also hate the show because it's depressing to think he's happy being single forever."

"Is he?" Avery swallowed a spike of pain. "Happy being single forever?" Maybe Sophie really was right to warn her away. Avery missed Geoff a surprising amount, but maybe she had made the right choice after all.

Sophie made a face. "It certainly feels like that sometimes. I mean, after our parents got divorced, Geoff kind of committed to this bachelor thing, and his show is another way of clinging to it. But I think, deep down, he wants that connection just as much as everyone else." She drummed her fingers over the hand mixer with a pensive look in her eyes. "I don't think he's there yet, Ave. Right now anyone who's with him is a fool if they think they're not going to get hurt. But I want him to figure it out eventually. I want him to find someone already and move on."

Avery frowned. "But if he found someone, that would mean quitting the show, wouldn't it? And that's his livelihood."

"Not necessarily. He could adapt. Evolve. I don't really know if you have to choose to walk away from the things you love. You just grow with them."

Avery pulled in a deep breath to chase away the tears that stung her eyes. Maybe she could have adapted for Geoff too, tried to be a little less scared, but it was too late for that now. "You are wise beyond your years, Soph."

Her friend grinned and held out the hand mixer. "I know. It's part of my charm." Her eyes held a wicked gleam. "Now get mixing, babe. These ingredients aren't going to cream themselves."

CHAPTER 14

"*E*xcuse me?"

Geoff looked up from his beer and into the face of a pretty blonde. Her eyes were narrowed in concentration, and a smile graced her lips.

"You're him, aren't you?" Beside the blonde, her friend watched the exchange with an amused smile.

Geoff cocked his head and smiled back.

Across the table of Capitol Hill's Foreign National bar, Ryan answered for him. "I'm not sure who *him* is, but if *him* is handsome, successful, and ready for a good time, then you've found your man right here."

Geoff groaned. "Excuse my friend. He's a Neanderthal."

"And he clearly hasn't listened to your podcast, has he?"

Geoff lifted his eyebrows in surprise. "I suppose not." Maybe he hadn't given this girl enough credit.

"Ha!" She gave him a victorious smile. "I knew it was you. Geoff Carpenter from *How to Hook a Hottie*, right?"

He nodded. Carpenter, Carter. Close enough. "One and the same."

"I'm Michelle." Geoff shook the hand Michelle offered, and she shot him a look of shy flirtation. "Any chance I can get your autograph?"

"Sure." He accepted the paper coaster she held out to him, scrawling his name inside the Greek key border.

"Actually, my friend Stephanie had a relationship question for you. Any chance we can join you for a drink and have a minute to pick your brain?"

Geoff hesitated, and Ryan kicked him under the table. Ryan patted the empty chair beside him. "We would be thrilled."

The one thing about being a podcaster was that Geoff was famous enough online, but most people didn't notice him when he went out in public, so he could fly under the radar. It was the best of both worlds. Still, there were added benefits to being considered a dating expert during those times when someone did spot him in a crowd.

"Great!" Michelle and Stephanie perched at their table, shoving out their breasts and batting their eyelashes. Normally Geoff would have paid attention, but today he didn't quite have the heart. He did his best to answer their questions, but all he wanted to do was get the hell out of here. What was wrong with him tonight?

He waited for what seemed like a polite amount of time before pushing his chair back from the table. "I'm sorry, ladies, but Ryan and I have another appointment this evening."

Michelle frowned. "Guess I should give you my autograph, too." She reached for another coaster and wrote down her name and number while Ryan peered over her shoulder and grinned.

Geoff gritted his teeth and ground out, "Nice to meet you," before hauling Ryan out to the street.

On the sidewalk, Ryan paused. "Forgetting something?"

"My dignity?" Geoff rubbed a hand over the back of his head and blew out a deep breath.

"Or a number." Ryan dangled Michelle's coaster from his fingers, and Geoff noticed she'd put a heart instead of a dot over the "i."

"I forgot."

Ryan shook his head. "You don't forget a pair of Ds like those three minutes later."

"It's not a big deal." Geoff scowled, but Ryan didn't seem to want to let it go.

"If this is how you handled yourself in New York, I'm not sure how you got so famous. You're like the cock-block of the century right now."

Geoff groaned. "I'm having a bad night, okay? Let's hit a different bar. I'll even let you keep that coaster." There was no way he was going to call Michelle-with-a-heart, anyway.

"No, I know what this is." Ryan rubbed his chin, his stubble rasping under his palm. "You're hung up on Avery. Didn't close the deal, did you?"

Geoff bristled. "Last I checked, it wasn't a transaction."

Ryan's face lit like an annoying little brother who'd just discovered blackmail material. "Denial's just a river in Egypt. You like her?"

He sighed. "Yeah, I guess I do."

"So why are you out with me instead of her?"

Because she hadn't said yes to a fourth date.

"Great question." A group of people dressed for the bar pushed past them, and noise from inside spilled out into the night, grating Geoff's ears. Why was he so damn sensitive tonight?

"Does she know how you feel?" Ryan asked.

"I thought so." He'd laid things out for Avery in the car before she bailed on him, but by that point, it seemed like she'd already made up her mind.

Ryan shot him a skeptical look. "Really?"

Geoff allowed for a margin of error. Women sometimes *were* creatures of a different breed. "Well...maybe."

"Dude, you need to let her know you're into her for more than the show. Make a stand. Be bold. Seize the day."

"Aren't you just an inspirational poster waiting to happen," Geoff said without heat.

Ryan shook his head. "I still don't know why I'm the one telling you these things."

"Maybe the problem's too close to home. I can't wrap my head around it." How could they go from the hot tub and talk of orgasms to...nothing?

Ryan clapped him on the shoulder and headed toward the bar's entrance.

"Where are you going?" Geoff asked.

"Back inside," Ryan called. "I'm going to console poor Michelle. You're going to go get your girl."

* * *

Avery swung open her apartment door wearing messy hair and a pair of tortoiseshell glasses that gave her a naughty librarian vibe. Her pajama shorts showed off curvy, toned legs, and her toenails were painted a pale purple—the color you found inside the shells of the muscles that lived in the Sound.

Her eyes went wide, and a wash of pink streaked over her cheeks. "Geoff." She twisted a bare foot into the carpet.

Geoff studied her face. "Is that 'Geoff' like 'yay?' Or 'Geoff' like 'crap?'"

She cracked a grin. "It's 'Geoff' like 'what are you doing here?'" She dropped her pretty eyes to the bag clutched in his hand. "Do you, um, need something for the show?"

"Actually, no." He held out the bag to her. "I was hoping we could talk."

Avery peered inside, smiling as she lifted out a sweating pint of strawberry ice cream and two plastic spoons. "Are you trying to get on my good side?"

"Maybe." He wiped a sweaty palm on the leg of his pants. "In fairness, I don't know if you have a bad side."

"O-kay," she said. "Definitely trying to bribe me." He opened his mouth to protest, and she laughed. "Come on in."

Inside her apartment, Avery grabbed a few paper towels from the roll on her kitchen counter and led Geoff to the couch. He took the spot next to her, shaking his head when she offered him a spoon. He was too nervous to eat, but what he wouldn't give to be her ice cream right now, the plastic spoon sucked clean in her mouth.

"So, what's up?" Avery asked around a mouthful of dessert.

"I've got a problem."

She lifted an eyebrow. "What's that?"

He cleared his throat and tried to find the right words. "I miss you, Cheese. I keep wanting to pick up my phone and call you, and then I keep feeling like I can't. Like the other day, I caught the Sounders game and wanted to pick up the phone just to say 'Will Bruin' and hear you laugh. But you ran off on me the other night."

She lowered her spoon uncertainly. "We're friends, Geoff."

He shook his head. "We're not."

She blinked at him. "Oh." A drop of melted ice cream splashed onto her coffee table, leaving behind a pale pink circle.

"I mean that's not what I want." He held her eyes, needing her to see how much he meant this. "I want to be with you, Avery. For real. Not for the show. Sometimes I feel like there's a whole layer of my life that I don't need to explain to you because you were already there. I can be comfortable with you, Ave, like we're picking up in a new place but we've got a lifetime of history between us."

It was the truth his mind kept spinning back to at home without her, at the bar without her, anywhere without her.

Her mouth dropped open. "But after the virginity thing…" She shook her head. "I thought you were just being nice about it after that."

"No, Avery, I was trying to be respectful." His hands trembled against his thighs. "I'd love to strip every piece of clothing off of you right now. Get my hands and mouth on you and not let go."

She sucked in a sharp breath. "I thought you didn't like me. That you were playing along because you had to."

"Nothing could be further from the truth. I more than like you, Avery."

She winced. "I'm sorry. I'm so bad at reading the signs." She shrugged. "Guess that's why I'm still single."

Geoff took a deep breath and looked into her clear, beautiful eyes. "Do you want to change that?"

CHAPTER 15

eoff looked so sincere, sitting on Avery's couch in his dark jeans and a button-down shirt, asking her for something more. His eyebrows drew together with the question, his voice so vulnerable and full of hope. Avery's heart leaped at the offer he held out to her, and the memory of every kiss with him stirred in her belly.

He wanted her.

He more than wanted her.

Her mind flashed back to all the little moments with him—those kisses, his arms around her to protect her from the crowd at the Sounders game, the look on his face when she'd flirted with the guy at the kayak rental stand.

He wasn't indifferent. He was jealous.

How could she have been so stupid?

"Are you sure?" she asked him with trembling lips. "Because there are probably a lot of girls out there who actually say the right thing at the right time. Unlike babbling when they're nervous. Which is what I'm doing now."

Oh, god, she was going to blow this.

Geoff just grinned. "You're perfect, Avery. And I love your mouth, no matter what it's saying." She snorted, and his smile widened. "I especially love it when it's calling my name. So what do you say, Cheese Girl? Yes or no?"

She smiled up at him. "Yes, Rock, yes. I really, really want this."

Geoff's features softened with relief, and he pulled her against him. Avery's hand landed over his heart, and his strong arms banded around her back. "God, Ave, you have no idea how much I wanted to hear that." He slanted his mouth over hers and pulled her so close she could feel his heart hammering in his chest, matching the beat of her own.

In Seattle it rained all the time, but real, huge thunderstorms—the kind with lightning and big, black clouds—were rare. This kiss felt like thunder rumbling before a summer storm, like the sky was going to break open and bring all the rain and relief that the world needed.

Avery leaned into Geoff's touch and moaned against him, opening her mouth and letting him in. Her mouth was cold from the ice cream, but he filled it with heat, his tongue demanding and dangerous as it explored hers. She let her eyes fall closed, shutting out the world and all the stupid reasons she'd run away from him before. He was here now, and for whatever reason, he'd picked her.

She wasn't going to walk away again.

Geoff deepened the kiss, controlling it while he tangled a hand in her hair. He guided her backward gently until she was spread on her couch, hot and needy. Avery hadn't worn a bra tonight, and her nipples tightened under her tank top. His eyes skimmed over them, landing on her face with a reverent look that made her feel desired and cherished at the same time.

"I like those glasses," he whispered. "But we should probably take them off."

"Mmm," she agreed. "Probably." She slipped them from her face and placed them on her side table, then brought her gaze back to Geoff. He looked so damn good, his eyes dark with arousal, his lips full and kissable.

And hers.

The thought made her chest heat, and a wave of desire washed over her. "Anything else you think we should take off?" she asked, shooting him a teasing look.

His voice came out low and surprised. "Whatever you're comfortable with, Ave. You set the pace."

She licked her lips and swallowed hard, then reached for the hem of her tank top. She lifted it up and over her head, then wiggled off her shorts. She lay there in only her underwear, her body an offering.

And Geoff looked at her like she was a prize.

"God, you're so beautiful." His voice was full of heat and awe. "Where have you been my whole life?"

She smiled back at him. "Right here." The perfect symmetry of the moment felt exactly right—Geoff who she'd always wanted, who she knew without starting from scratch. At least, she knew him in so many ways except this one. But this way—his tongue on her body, his hands in her hair —might be her favorite way of all.

Avery ran her fingers over the buttons of his shirt, pulling them open one by one. His shirt revealed inch after inch of tan skin, his toned chest beckoning to her. She'd follow that trail wherever it led.

Geoff helped her slide the material from his shoulders, then he reached for the button on his jeans. Avery's eyes widened as he unbuttoned them and slid them over his feet. He was left in just his boxers, his erection straining against the material. All for her.

She grinned and pulled him down to her, her hands roaming over the tight, firm muscles of his back. He was built like a statue, like someone had dreamed up the perfect man and delivered him right to her doorstep. Clothing optional.

"Lucky me," Geoff whispered into her hair.

He kissed her like the world was ending, his body on hers. This skin to skin sensation was so very, very good, and she was lost to him.

Avery groaned as Geoff's erection pressed against her hip, moving her body so she could grind against it. She arched her back, pressing her chest against his, the soft hair on his chest brushing against her nipples.

He pulled back, breathing heavy. "Jesus, Ave, what are you doing to me?"

She laughed. "You tell me. Pretty sure you're the one who's got more experience here."

"Tempting the hell out of me, Ave."

She bit her lip. "You don't need to hold back, Geoff. I'm yours." It was true even when she'd pushed him away, but here, tonight—together—she'd never meant it more.

Geoff smiled, but rather than reaching for her again he picked up one of the plastic spoons from the coffee table. Avery rolled up onto her elbow, breathless, and narrowed her eyes. "You're hungry now?"

He gave her a dark, sensual look. "I'm starved."

"Oh." The air puffed out of her, and she giggled as he pushed her gently back onto the couch. Then he reached for the ice cream and scooped out a spoonful.

He dropped it into her bellybutton, licking the spoon before setting it back into the pint of ice cream. Avery shrieked at the cold and wiggled her hips, causing a trail of melted ice cream to spill toward the couch.

"Catch it!" she squealed.

Geoff held her still with a hand on the opposite hip, dropping his mouth to the ice cream and licking it clean. The heat of his tongue replaced the cool ice cream, and sensation spiraled across her skin—heat and cold, the gentle tickle of the ice cream and the steady insistence of his tongue. The stubble on his chin scraped across her tender skin, and every nerve in her body lit on fire.

Oh.

"Are you going to worry about your couch?" he growled. "Or are you going to let me eat my fill?"

She shook her head and smiled, her heart trying to burst free from her chest. "Ruin the damn couch for all I care. Just keep going."

"Good girl."

Geoff swirled his tongue into her bellybutton, lapping at the ice cream, and Avery's body sang with awareness, her clit begging for attention.

He sat up and spooned another scoop of ice cream. This time he drew the spoon lower, dripping a trail of melting ice cream from her belly button south, the final spill pooling just above the elastic of her underwear.

He lowered his mouth, kissing and sucking his way down, then finally pushing her underwear down her thighs.

He drew in a deep breath. "So beautiful," he murmured. His words were warm on her clit, and then so was his tongue.

Avery gasped as his lips grazed her most sensitive skin. "That feels so good, Geoff."

"Good." He stroked his tongue over her, and her hips bucked for him. "You deserve every bit of pleasure I can give you."

He kept up his sweet attention, licking and sucking like he really was getting his damn fill, and her apartment filled with the sound of her heavy breathing, her moans as he coaxed her higher and higher.

Avery scraped a hand through Geoff's hair, pulling him closer, her hips churning shamelessly now. Her body tingled, so very close to the peak of this mountain. She was going to jump off the top. She was never going to touch the ground.

"I'm going to come, Geoff," she whispered, and he smiled against her clit, pushing a finger inside her.

Then two.

The dual sensation—his tongue outside of her, his fingers inside— pushed Avery to the edge, and her heart was in her mouth, and her body was pure sensation, and there was nothing in the world except his hot, skilled tongue, stroking her into oblivion.

"I'm going to—" and then she was crying out wordlessly, her body wracked by an orgasm so strong there were no thoughts anymore, nothing but pleasure. It tumbled through her like an avalanche, reverberating all the way into her heart.

Oh god.

Oh, holy shit.

Geoff.

He pulled his hands from her, smoothing a kiss high on her inner thigh before drawing up on the couch alongside her. He pressed a kiss against the arch of her neck, then whispered in her ear. "You're right, Ave. Your orgasm face might be my very favorite."

She felt flushed and wild, so beautiful and adored.

She smiled at him, and he smiled back at her. "Imagine that."

Her body was looser, more relaxed now, but Geoff's erection still pressed against her side. Avery reached a hand down, skimming a finger along the waistband of his boxers. Then further down, underneath the fabric, until she could wrap her hand around him.

"But what does *your* orgasm face look like, I wonder?" Her voice came out so breathy, still so aroused.

Geoff groaned and closed his eyes, the pleasure and concentration on his face making her feel like a goddess. Powerful. His beautiful eyelashes pitched dark against his skin, and when she and Geoff were like this, so close and wrapped up together, his features transformed into bliss.

This was going to be the face she remembered for the rest of her life.

This secret side of him that she hadn't known before.

She wanted it.

She wanted him.

Avery stroked her hand around him, pulling another groan from him, his body hot and hard in her hand.

"I'm pretty sure you're making every one of my high school fantasies come true right now," he confessed.

She couldn't help her proud smile. "You fantasized about me?"

"All the damn time."

He tugged her mouth toward him, kissed her so deeply that he left her breathless, her mouth so tender it was almost bruised. All the blood in her body raced straight back between her thighs, and she squeezed him gently, flicked a finger over the soft velvet head.

He groaned again and pulled away, breathing heavy. "What do you want?"

"You," she whispered. She needed him—needed this connection—and she wouldn't be satisfied until she'd had everything he could give her. "More of you."

Geoff stroked a hand over the side of her face. "Then come to the bedroom, Ave. I want you to be comfortable."

She nodded, her throat suddenly dry. "Yes." This was what she wanted. "Okay."

Geoff stood and pushed his boxers to his feet, and the full sight of his erection made her swoon. He had a huge, perfect cock—strong and thick—

something even better than the toy design team at work could have dreamed up.

Avery's eyes widened, and she bit back a grin.

"Like what you see?"

"Very, very much. Guess I should have been calling you Rock all along."

Geoff's low, pleased laugh rumbled in her stomach. He reached for her hand and pulled her to her feet. "Come on, Cheese. I need to get my hands back on your body as soon as I can."

She giggled and led him to her bedroom, anticipation clenching every muscle in her body tight. Geoff kissed her at the foot of her bed and then on top of it, tangling his limbs with hers. Then he helped her toward the pillows and stroked a hand between her legs.

"So wet for me, Avery."

"Yes," she panted, wrapping a hand around him. "All for you."

He dipped a finger inside her, drew her arousal onto her clit and circled his finger so all the sensation in her body swirled onto that tiny bundle of nerves. "You're going to be sore, Ave."

"I can handle it. Please, please come inside me."

He held her eye, so sincere she lost her breath. "Are you sure?"

"I'm sure."

He nodded and pressed a gentle kiss to her mouth. "Condom?"

She nodded her head toward her bedside table, and as he reached for a foil packet and rolled the condom over his length, she couldn't help but want to laugh. This was not how she'd seen tonight going when she'd opened the door to him, but this is exactly how she wanted it now.

Geoffrey Carter.

No longer untouchable, unattainable. Just hers, tonight, here and now.

Geoff returned to the bed, balancing on his forearms above her, and his solid knee nudged hers apart.

She parted for him, sighed as he rubbed himself at her entrance.

"This okay, Ave?"

"More," she whispered, her heart in her mouth, and he eased inside.

Geoff moved slowly, entering her inch by inch. He was bigger than any toy she'd ever brought home from work, and the fullness was almost overwhelming. He stroked her from the inside, bringing such perfect pleasure that her eyes fluttered closed. Why had she waited so long for this? It was magic, it was fire, every plane of their bodies connected, just sparking together.

She was claimed.

She was his.

And he was hers.

Geoff reached the end, so fully inside of her, breathing heavy while he allowed her to adjust. Avery rocked against him slowly, feeling for the edges of this sensation, finding her comfort.

"Okay?" he asked again, and she nodded. "Good girl. Just remember to breathe. It makes everything better."

She opened her eyes and laughed against him. "I'll try."

Slowly he made love to her, his face buried in her neck, his hands holding her, protecting her, his mouth whispering how very much this meant to him.

And as they moved together, rocking faster now, Avery realized it wasn't just her surrendering. It was both of them coming undone, making something fresh and whole with their eager bodies. Something beautiful and new forming in the space of their breath.

She slipped a hand over his shoulders and pulled him tighter, closer, and he pushed her higher with every stroke. She could feel the heat gathering again, her body quickening.

"I'm going to come," Avery whispered, and he lifted his head, stared into her eyes.

"I want to see your face again." Geoff churned his hips, cradled the back of her head. "Keep your eyes open, gorgeous."

It was so damn hard not to close them, but she made herself stare into his dark brown gaze, so warm and familiar, but so different now, too.

"I'm going to come, too, sweetheart." And he was pumping now, faster and faster, all his restraint from before gone as he chased this orgasm. Geoff's forehead creased in concentration, and each stroke plunged deeper, hit every nerve ending inside Avery's body.

She came before she could warn him, calling out his name. "Geoff!" she cried as he brought her over the edge, her body exploding with light.

He came along with her, a low groan, and his eyes so open and honest. "Oh, god, Avery," he moaned, pumping, extending her orgasm, making her vision fill with stars. "Thank you."

He kissed her gently, then searched her eyes. "Was that okay for you?"

"More than okay." Her heart raced as she grinned back at him, tapped a hand against his chest. "When can we do that again?"

CHAPTER 16

*G*eoff woke in Avery's bed with her hair tickling his cheek and her soft body pressed against his, all heat and promise. Her eyes were already open, sleepy but satisfied, and for the first time since he'd moved back to Seattle, he had the feeling that he was exactly where he was supposed to be.

"Morning, Cheese." He pressed a kiss to the side of her head, breathing in her sweet shampoo. She'd showered last night before climbing into bed, but the scent of strawberries still hung in the air.

"Morning to you, too."

"Feel okay?"

Avery grinned. "Never better. I feel incredible." She stretched against him, and his cock perked up at the invitation. "Like I could touch anything and turn it into pure gold."

"That's why they call it getting lucky."

She giggled and stroked a hand over his chest. "Maybe we should buy Lotto tickets."

"Sign me up." He shifted her body so he was facing her, then stroked his hand over her hip. Avery had pulled on a camisole last night, but it left little to the imagination, and as he touched her, he watched her nipples bead up into little peaks.

He'd been there.

Claimed her.

And he wanted to do it again.

"I don't want this to sound wrong," Geoff said, "but I can't believe you haven't done that before."

She gave a tiny shrug, not self-conscious, just self-explanatory. "I've gotten close. Done everything but. I had this boyfriend back in college, and things were pretty serious. The night I was finally ready to give it up to him, I planned a whole thing. Cooked dinner at his apartment as a surprise, lit candles. Tried to be romantic."

Geoff nodded, not wanting to break her train of thought with his words. And anyway, what could he say? He didn't want to hear the end of the story, even though he could guess how it turned out.

"He showed up at the apartment with another girl. Looked like he was going to vomit when he realized I was there to surprise him." Avery shook her head. "Thank god it wasn't him. But after that…" She sighed. "I guess I got a little gun shy, and then it became this bigger thing in my head. I put more pressure on it than was really fair. Maybe tried too hard." She laughed. "I mean, I'm surrounded by sex on a daily basis. It's my job. And I like it. I just didn't have first-hand experience."

He nuzzled the side of her neck. "Until now."

She smiled and brought her nose against his. "Until now."

Avery's kiss made his cock twitch, the sounds she made sealing the deal.

Geoff tugged a hand through her hair and pulled gently, so she was looking him in the eye. "Your ex-boyfriend? He was an idiot."

She blushed and nodded. "He was."

"Let me show you just how much." He trailed his hand from her hip to the edge of her underwear, and she shivered at his touch. "You sore?" he asked.

Avery bit her lip and then grinned. "Of course I'm sore. You're a rock, remember?"

He shook his head. "What am I going to do with you?"

"You're going to fuck me again." Avery's eyes darkened with arousal, and she nodded like this was a very good idea.

"But you're sore."

"This is true. I'm also horny as hell, and you're half naked in my bed. I don't see the problem."

This woman. She'd been hiding behind the tongue-tied girl he used to know. Geoff grinned back at her and dipped a finger inside her slit. "I think I unleashed a monster."

Avery arched against his hand. "Or a superhero, whatever." She closed her eyes as he stroked inside her, a soft moan sending more blood to his cock. He let out a deep breath, and she opened her eyes with a smile. "You okay, Rock?"

"The sounds you make might just kill me."

She reached for him, rubbing him through the fabric of his boxers. "But what a way to go."

Geoff leaned forward to kiss her, and as the kiss deepened into a heady, sensual touch, its intensity grew. He was circling her clit, she was jacking him with her hands, her breasts bouncing under her shirt, and good god, he really was eighteen again, all his fantasies come to life.

But then Avery pulled back from him, pulled out of reach and pushed him flat on his back.

She slid to the end of the bed and removed his boxers, then crawled back to him on her hands and knees. She stopped between his legs, gave him a racy smile, and then lowered her mouth to his cock.

Hell fucking yes.

Avery's lips circled him, and her tongue darted out to taste him. Her touch started as slow, gentle strokes with her tongue, but when she pulled him deep into the back of her mouth and sucked hard, Geoff realized her first touches weren't tentative. She'd just been letting him warm up.

And, Jesus Christ, was he up.

He relaxed into her touch, his eyes drifting closed as she worked him with her tongue and her hands. "That feels incredible, Avery."

She moved her mouth away long enough to tell him how good he tasted, then brought that damp heat and suction back to his skin. Every nerve ending screamed for release, and his hips churned for her, his heart beat for her.

Geoff reached for her the back of her head and pulled her closer, fisting his hands into her hair. All of his awareness was centered on her mouth around his cock. A robber could have burst through Avery's apartment doors and stolen all of their earthly possessions, and he wouldn't have known the difference.

He was right here with her.

Until he felt his balls tighten.

"Not yet, Ave," Geoff gasped, pulling away. She murmured a protest, and he opened his eyes to shoot her a look. "I want to be inside you."

She gave him a pleased smile. "We can arrange that."

"Good girl." He turned to reach for the drawer on her bedside table and removed a condom from the drawer.

Avery took it from his hands, opened it and rolled it onto him, her fingers so eager that they shook.

"Want to try something different than last night?" he asked.

"I want to try all the things," she said breathlessly. "Everything with you."

He grinned. "I like the sound of that." He wanted to try all the positions in the damn book with her, and make up a hundred new ones, too. But he'd start at the beginning. The classics were classic for a reason. "On your knees, gorgeous."

Avery complied, lifting her ass into the air and waiting while he climbed behind her. She looked over her shoulder at him, watching with huge eyes as he gripped the base of his cock and positioned himself at her entrance.

Geoff pushed himself against her lips, teasing her, wanting her wet and ready for him to ease the pain. "You sure you're not too sore?"

"I'm sure if you don't keep going I'm going to lose my mind."

"We wouldn't want that," he said as he slid inside her.

"No," she gasped, "we wouldn't." A low moan rolled through her, and he smoothed a hand over her ass, pushing in deeper, inch by inch.

Her greedy cunt took him all the way to the root, rippling around him, and Geoff almost lost it right there. Nirvana was a place, and it was balls-deep inside Avery Beeker's body. No return ticket necessary.

"Okay?" he asked.

"Yes," she cried. "Sore but very, very okay. You're so damn deep."

Her words made him that much harder. "Touch yourself." The gruff command tore from his throat. "I want to feel you squeeze me as you come."

Her moan was an acknowledgment, a submittal. She brought one hand between her legs and braced herself against the headboard with the other.

Geoff pulled out and then pushed back in, letting Avery sheath him. The sensation of her tight, hot body made him groan, the air rushing out of his lungs so he was lightheaded—dizzy and drunk on her.

"Harder, Rock," she panted, and hearing that nickname made him tighten even more. "You're not going to break me," she promised, but god he wanted to try.

He thrust into her again and again, and her body jerked beneath him, her ass slapping against his thighs, their bodies growing slick with arousal and sweat. He reached one hand for her breasts, kneading them as they bounced with the rhythm of their sex, and she moaned as he tightened his fingers around a nipple.

"You're going to make me come," she breathed.

"That's exactly the point."

Geoff kept up the barrage, fingers flying over her breasts, his other hand kneading her ass, guiding her, and her legs tightened and her sex quivered and then she was calling out, pulling him over the edge along with her so they were one body, shimmering with light and magic as the world fell away.

After a minute, Avery's body quieted, and he rested his forehead on her back, his chest still rising and falling with ragged breath.

"Oh, fuck, Ave."

"I know."

He pulled out of her, wrapped an arm around her and drew her against his chest, down on the bed. He pressed a kiss against her temple, then lower, behind her ear. The scent of strawberries and shampoo and sex was everywhere, and it might be the best combination he'd ever smelled.

Avery threw a luscious leg over his, gave him a lazy smile.

"Still okay?" he asked.

"Still golden." But her features twisted, her mouth pulling into a tiny frown.

"Hey, what's wrong?"

She shook her head like she was trying to clear away a thought. "Is it stupid that I'm jealous of every other girl who got to do that with you?"

Geoff laced his fingers with hers and tugged them to his lips. "Trust me, Ave, it hasn't been like that with anyone else. You and me, that's...different."

She gave him a small, pleased smile. "Good. Well, I'm not going to lie, you've wiped me out today."

He grinned and kissed her forehead. "Go back to bed, and I can catch up on some work from here."

She gave him such a hopeful look. "You sure?"

"I'm sure, Cheese Girl. Get some rest. I've got plans for you later." He kissed her shoulder and slipped out of the room.

Geoff padded out into Avery's living room, which looked exactly like they'd left it last night—complete with the ice cream container sitting out on her coffee table.

Oh shit. He lifted it and discovered the melted ice cream had softened the carton's sides into a soggy mess.

Oh well. Best ice cream he'd ever tasted.

He poured the soupy ice cream down the drain in Avery's kitchen, then tossed away the carton and ran a damp rag over her coffee table. When he'd cleaned up enough to pass muster, he stretched out on the couch and dove into emails on his phone.

The benefit of working for yourself was you could work from anywhere, and today was no exception. One of his sponsors, Slay All Night, had sent him a message. *Re: new season opportunities.*

Geoff skimmed the message, and his heart sank. In theory, new season opportunities were a good thing. Hell, sponsor advertisements were one of the largest revenue streams for his show. But Slay All Night, the hookup app, wanted assurances that they'd have roughly the same audience demographics and the same variety of episodes in the upcoming months. Geoff was going to lose major advertising dollars if he didn't deliver the kind of content he was already known for. And since he was known as the single-guy dating expert, that meant keeping a lid on this thing with Avery—at least until he could figure out what it meant for his show. And for his life.

Geoff sighed and typed back a message. Once he sorted out where he stood, he could adapt and adjust. In the meantime, he was going to proceed in his business like he always had. He was Geoffrey Carter, host of *How to Hook a Hottie*. He had a reputation to maintain. His living counted on it.

CHAPTER 17

*a*very shifted her purse onto her shoulder, adjusting the bag of sex toys she'd brought home from work in her hands as she turned the key in her apartment's mailbox. It was an awkward angle, and the one-handed approach didn't work. Her mail spilled out of her grasp, a stack of bills and grocery store flyers scattering on the tile floor.

Better mail than sex toys.

Those she had plans for.

She bent down to scoop up the dropped envelopes, rifling through them until her fingers hit a thick, deep-blue envelope with her name calligraphed on the front in silver ink.

Oh.

Avery straightened and hurried into her apartment, lowering her purse and the sex toys onto her couch. Then she slit open the blue envelope and gasped as a wedding invitation fell into her hands. The creamy paper was thick and textured, and the design scrolling across the page was simple but elegant.

Miss Vanessa Reese and Mr. Jeremy Glass warmly request the honor of your presence at their wedding on Saturday, November 17 at the Arctic Club Hotel. Ceremony at 5 PM, reception to follow.

The wedding logo, a birch tree with their initials twined over the leaves, crested the top of both the invitation and the enclosed reply card.

Avery skimmed the note.

They'd invited her and a plus one.

She drew in a deep breath. Her fingers twitched to dial Geoff, to ask him right now to be her date. The idea of him in a suit made her press her thighs together in anticipation.

But just because she wanted to ask him didn't mean it was a good idea. They'd barely started this relationship, but it felt so deep, so intense—like they'd been building to this all along. She knew, though, that back in high school she wouldn't have been ready for him. She was too worried about being the person everyone else wanted, not confident enough to be fully herself. But Geoff had drawn that part out of her, all the awkward quirks that seemed to endear her to him instead of pushing him away.

Telling him about her ex should have felt like an embarrassment, but it felt solid and mature instead. Geoff deserved to know her, the way he was letting her in as well. And she was giving him every part of herself, letting him see her without makeup, without clothes. Skin to skin was about as real as you could get.

Either way, the whole thing had been worth the wait. Sex with Geoff was mind-bending. Paradigm-shifting. There was before and there was after, and Geoff was the constant that carried her through.

Avery walked into her kitchen and dropped the envelope onto her counter. She still had time to respond to the invitation. She could let it sit for a day. First, she had some work to do.

* * *

A KNOCK SOUNDED on Avery's door, and she glanced up sharply. Was it seven o'clock already? The last few hours had flown by.

She moved her laptop off her knees, setting it on the edge of the coffee table and rushing toward the door. She swung it open, and her breath flew out at the sight of Geoff in a dark green long-sleeved T-shirt that drew out the color of his eyes. His expression was deeply pleased, and her body thrilled in his presence. She wanted to lean forward and kiss him, so she did.

She could do things like that now.

How lucky was she?

Geoff grinned against her mouth. "Nice to see you, too." He smelled like a warm, rich cologne, and she drew in a deep breath.

"Want to come in?"

"Thought you'd never ask."

Avery led him into the living room, and he stopped short of her couch, his eyes wide.

"What?" She followed his gaze to the sight of all her sex toys lined up on the coffee table. "Oh."

Geoff gave a low, heated laugh. "Is this like a *Choose Your Own Adventure* story?"

Avery waved her hands at the table. "Sorry, just got caught up in work things. I'm doing a roundup blog post of some of our favorite toys for couples to push to a few of the top industry blogs and publications."

"Is it so wrong that I want to get caught up in your work things, too?"

She bit her lip and tried to read his face. "Seriously?"

"Yeah, seriously, Cheese Girl. Show me what you've got."

She grinned. This probably wasn't following her own advice that she'd doled out on his show, but who the hell cared? She was a grown-ass woman who worked in the adult products industry, and she had a boyfriend who wanted to play. "You asked for it. First up, we've got a wand massager which is great for massaging, well, everything. But we all know that it's going straight between a woman's legs. It's super powerful and definitely a fan favorite for a reason."

Geoff raised an eyebrow. "You've tried that one?"

She tried to hide her smile. "I might have done my due diligence."

His growl of appreciation made her skin heat.

"Next up we have a vibrating cock ring. It's designed to keep you harder longer and make a more intense orgasm. It's also got a clit stimulator, so when a guy thrusts, it'll stimulate the woman's clit."

"Sounds like winning for everyone."

"In theory. I don't have a cock, so I haven't personally taken it for a spin." Avery pointed at the table. "Last up for this batch is the couples' wearable vibrator. It's worn inside during sex, and it stimulates the woman's G-spot, along with providing vibrations for the guy's shaft. This one's quiet, but it'll make you scream."

"Oh my god, Ave."

She laughed. "That's just the marketing text."

"I see why the people at your job like you so much."

She rolled her eyes. "It comes with the territory."

"Yeah, well, I like the way you think." Geoff drew her close, a hand sliding down her spine to cup her ass.

Avery blushed. "Thank you." Her phone chirped an interruption before she could say more, and she wrinkled her nose. "Let me get that and turn off the phone."

Geoff nipped her earlobe, sending a shock of arousal through her body. "Good plan."

She stepped out of his embrace to silence her phone, frowning when she read the text on the screen.

"Everything okay?" Geoff asked from his spot on the couch.

Avery held up her phone. "Your sister wants to know where I've been all weekend. What do I say?"

An unreadable look crossed his face, and he ran a hand over his forehead. "You might have been right about Sophie," he admitted.

"What do you mean?" Avery's stomach gave a weird, queasy lurch.

"We should probably keep this on the quiet side for now. Until we figure out how to break it to her."

She frowned. "We don't just say, 'Hey, Soph, we're together now, get over it?'"

Geoff repeated her own points back to her. "If I tell her, she'll cut off my balls because she thinks I'm going to hurt you."

Avery's chin trembled. "Are you?" Maybe Sophie was right. He was a player. But no, she couldn't think like that now. She'd said yes to Geoff, and she needed to give this thing a chance.

"No," he promised, "I'm not going to hurt you."

Relief stretched her mouth into a grin. "Good. So there you go," she said.

"Sure. But if you tell Sophie, she's going to think you've gone behind her back."

Avery winced. He had a point. "Fine. You're right." She gave a long sigh. "I'll just tell her I was working."

He grinned at her. "I mean, that's what you're going to do now, isn't it?"

She raised an eyebrow at the teasing tone in his voice. "Am I?"

"Yep. Product research. So you can write about that cock ring with an authoritative voice once and for all."

Avery's skin tingled, and a rush of warmth flowed straight to her core. Geoff climbed to his feet and stepped forward. His strong arms pulled her close once more, guiding her hips against an erection so hard she gasped.

"Working," she murmured, and then her voice was lost as he kissed away her words.

She dropped her phone onto the couch as he plucked the cock ring from her table and led her to the bedroom, the text forgotten, a message never sent.

CHAPTER 18

*A*very slipped through Geoff's front door on Friday night wearing her work clothes and carrying a bottle of wine.

"Oh my god, what smells so good?" She handed him the wine and slipped out of her heels by the front door, padding barefoot through his house toward the kitchen. She'd changed out her toenail polish—this time to white with polka dots. The flurry of color made Geoff smile. With every piece of professional clothing she slipped off, she got closer and closer to the girl he was falling for. Not that the pencil skirt and silky blouse combo was a bad look for her. Hell, the outfit showed off her legs and her curves, the top dipping just low enough to entice him without being garish.

"Dinner smells so good," he promised, watching her ass sway as she walked. In the kitchen, he uncorked the wine and poured two glasses, handing her one with a smile.

"Can I help you cook?" Avery asked.

"I think I've got it under control. "

She smiled. "Did Sophie give you aphrodisiac cooking lessons after all?"

"What?" He shook his head. "Hell, no. I'm a damned good cook all on my own. Sophie and I both had to step up after my parents got divorced, so I've been awesome from a young age." He nodded toward his barstools and

Avery sat, taking a deep draw of her wine. "And if I remember correctly, you like Italian food."

"You remember that from our date?"

"From that." He grinned at her. "And from the time you and Sophie cooked six of Ina Garten's pasta recipes in one day."

"Aww, I love Barefoot Contessa." Avery traced a finger over the mouth of the glass. "Though if we're being accurate to memory, I'm pretty sure Sophie did most of the cooking. I was just sous chef."

"Either way. I think I ate leftover noodles for a week straight."

"There are worse things."

Geoff nodded. "It's true. Anyway, in honor of that, I'm making you a weeknight bolognese with pappardelle and a crusty Italian loaf."

Avery's lips parted on a soft moan. "That sounds incredible."

"Good." He sipped his wine, the alcohol and the heat of the kitchen loosening his muscles. He wanted everything to be incredible for her—wanted to give her a reason to stay.

Avery took another sip of her wine, then set her glass on the kitchen counter. She glanced over her shoulder at his dining room table. "Tell you what, if you're doing all the cooking, I'm going to set the table."

Shit. He'd left a mess out there, too concerned about starting the sauce on time to clean up the work gear that covered the surface of the table.

Geoff shook his head and stirred the sauce. "I don't want you to lift a finger."

Avery smiled at him. "I'll just consider it a warm-up. Don't want to let my fingers get too lazy." She lowered her voice to a husky purr. "I might need them later tonight. And my mouth. And my tongue."

If she was going to demand to set the table and give him an excuse like that, well damn. Geoff tilted his head at her. "If it makes you happy."

Avery nodded. "Good." She slid off her stool and walked into the dining room, and he turned his attention back to the food. He gave the sauce another quick stir, wafting the scent of sirloin, tomatoes, and basil through his apartment.

"Just about ready," he called. Then he pulled the Italian loaf from his oven where it had been warming and set it on a cutting board until it was cool enough to handle.

"Um, hey."

Geoff froze at the uncertainty in Avery's voice, turning to face her.

"Where should I put these?" Avery clutched a stack of papers in her hands, work notes he'd jotted late last night after he'd gotten programming feedback from Slay All Night. Judging from the frown on her face, she'd seen them, too.

"In my studio is fine." He tried to play it off like no big deal, but the frown on her face didn't budge.

"Right." Her voice was a dry whisper. She slinked away into his studio, returning a minute later empty-handed. Her face was pinched, her eyes worried.

Avery blew out a deep breath. "So, I know we agreed to keep this thing between us a secret from Sophie, but I didn't realize it applied to your show, too."

Geoff's chest tightened, and his voice came out thick. "It's just for a little while, okay? I'm trying to sort out my work life, but this isn't personal."

She wrung her hands together. "Sure."

He set his wooden stirring spoon on a plate and walked around the counter to her. He took her hands in his and squeezed gently, so she looked in his eyes. "I'm all in, Avery."

Her eyes widened, her cheeks the prettiest pink. "But won't your listeners realize that you're, um…" Her eyes drifted away.

"Seeing someone?"

"Yeah."

"I've got a programming break right now, and I'm figuring out where I go from here. This wasn't part of my plan, Ave."

Her shoulders stiffened. "Am I a burden for you?"

"No." She needed to see that this was new for him too. Avery had been right when she called him out the other day. He hadn't been long-term material up until now, and maybe that was because he was still too fucked up by his parents' divorce. Or, maybe—and this possibility came deeper still —it was only because no one else had been her. Now that she was here, in his home, her laughter filling his life, he could look toward the future with her. And it looked pretty damn good. But she couldn't go cold on him now.

"You're everything, Cheese Girl. Just give me some time."

Avery lifted her eyes back to his, chewed on her lower lip. "Does that make this a good or bad time to tell you I got a wedding invitation from my boss?"

Geoff's shoulders stiffened, and he cocked his head at her. "I don't know."

"I got a plus one invite," she said.

"Oh. Right." His stomach clenched at the idea. "Weddings, huh?"

She nodded. "Weddings." She looked at him hopefully. "Would you be my date? It's in November, so if that's too far out, I totally get it..." She spoke quickly, the way she did when she was nervous, and Geoff wanted to ease her mind even though everything in his body shouted to run.

He swallowed a spike of panic. "Going to a wedding is kind of like symbolizing the death of a single man."

Her face went red, and she pulled her hands from his. "But you're not single anymore. Unless I totally misunderstood everything."

He blew out a breath. "No, you're right Ave. I'm just, you know, trying to break my old programming." He rubbed a hand over the back of his head. "I think seeing my parents get divorced kind of threw me for a loop, you know. My world got totally upended, and my dad bailed to who the hell knows where. It kind of tore everything apart, and I don't know if I ever really recovered from that."

"Does that mean you don't believe in weddings?"

"A wedding's just a fancy party, right?" He gave her a confident smile. "I can do that."

"But I mean, do you believe in marriage?"

Dammit.

Geoff's chest felt heavy. He'd been a dating expert for over three years, and he still didn't know if happily ever after was possible. At the same time, what he'd said to Avery that night in the car was still true—he didn't know where this would lead, but he was willing to see it through.

Geoff cleared his throat. "I believe that it's possible to find the right person who makes you want to wake up every day and keep choosing her. I believe that with the right person you can be happy for a lifetime."

"Oh." Avery pressed her lips into a smile, and her eyelashes fluttered. "That's a really good answer."

Geoff forced a smile. "Good. And it's a yes, Ave. We can make it happen. Let's go to a wedding."

"Really?" Her voice was so damn hopeful—he couldn't disappoint her now.

"Sure, Cheese. I want to see you in a fancy dress. As long as I get to peel it off of you afterward."

"Deal."

He was going to do this for her. He had to.

Nerves churned Geoff's stomach like an ocean in gale-force winds, but the sparkle in Avery's eyes almost crowded out his fears.

Almost.

But not quite.

CHAPTER 19

*A*very woke in Geoff's bed, the whole of Seattle spread right outside the window. The day was dark and close, October in the Pacific Northwest with an undercurrent of rain. She nestled deeper under the covers, snuggling against the warmth radiating from Geoff's skin. His chest stretched solid like a comfort, and he brushed a hand down her back.

"Morning, gorgeous," he whispered.

"Morning to you, too." It felt so easy to fall into him, to let him kiss her awake, and she let all the strain of yesterday fade away. Who cared that he'd turned the color of a sheet of paper when she'd first asked him to go to the wedding? He'd said yes, and maybe he could get past whatever was spooking him.

And if it was the divorce, well, Sophie was getting past it.

Geoff would, too.

Avery propped her chin on his chest, smiling at the way the soft hair on his pecs tickled her chin. "I feel pretty spoiled from that dinner yesterday. Any objections to me making you breakfast?"

He stroked a lazy hand through her hair, his fingertips on her scalp sending warm tingles through her body. This was what cats must feel like. No wonder they were always so smug about life. "I'm not going to complain about it," he said.

"Good." Avery grinned at him and slipped out of his arms. She was still naked from last night when they'd had each other for dessert. They'd topped off the whole affair with the fresh gingerbread cookies Geoff had baked for her, eaten warm in his bed.

He was definitely spoiling her.

Avery pulled open his drawer and slipped one of his T-shirts over her head. He'd worn this back in high school, and she felt like such a fucking grown-up as she wore it now. Then she spun into his kitchen, sorting through the ingredients in his fridge.

She pulled flour, sugar, eggs, and milk onto his counter, then reached around in his pantry to see what else she could rustle up.

Chocolate chips.

Bingo.

Avery found a recipe for pancakes on Sophie's Instagram feed, then mixed the batter while she heated a frying pan on Geoff's stove. This was going to be a good surprise.

She poured a few scoops of batter into the pan, the sizzle heating her face and the smell of sugar wafting through his apartment. She was on the last batch of pancakes when Geoff's voice drifted over her shoulder.

"Oh my god, what smells like heaven?" Geoff walked up behind her and wrapped his arms around her waist. "Chocolate chip pancakes?" He moved her hair aside and pressed a kiss to the crook of her neck.

Avery giggled. "Obviously. If you don't make me burn them."

Bubbles appeared in the pancakes on the griddle, and she flipped them, smiling way more than necessary.

Geoff grabbed one of the finished ones off the plate with his fingers and ripped it in two. He fed Avery half, then took a bite of his half and chewed thoughtfully.

"So good." He kissed her neck again and brought his hands back to her waist. She liked this connection, the feeling that he couldn't keep his hands off of her. She felt bold and proud, sexy and wanted. And for the first time in her life, it was for all of her. Not just the side of her she showed the rest of the world.

"You know," Geoff said, "the first time I ever saw you it was over a plate of chocolate chip pancakes."

Avery stilled, her mouth dropping open. He'd remembered. "Really?" she whispered, and Geoff nodded.

"Sophie must have had you over for some sleepover, but I'd been out late and didn't know until I came down to breakfast the next morning. My mom had made pancakes, and you and Sophie were sitting there, looking ready to eat the whole kitchen." Avery scoffed. "You were cute, Cheese Girl, but after I asked you to pass the syrup, you didn't say a word for the rest of breakfast."

She giggled, remembering. "It was probably safer that way. We all know that when I open my mouth, there's no saying what will come out."

"As I told you before, I like your mouth."

She grinned at him and flipped off the burner. "It really is such a mystery to me that I'm so good with writing. But I guess practice makes perfect."

"Hmm." Geoff took another bite of his stolen pancake. "Honest to god, every time I eat these I think of you."

"I guess I should make more of them." She wrapped her arms around his neck and sealed his mouth in a kiss that tasted like chocolate.

"You should. But let's be real, the pancakes are just a vehicle for the chocolate."

Avery blinked her eyes at him, a picture of mock innocence.

Geoff grinned and lifted the finished serving plate of food. "Sugar for breakfast. You might try to look all healthy for the rest of the world, but I'm on to you, Cheese Girl."

"I have a feeling you are."

Avery followed Geoff into his dining room, where light from the windows spilled onto his wide, beautiful table. He set the plate on the table and gestured at the pancakes. "Mind if I post a picture of these to my Instagram feed?"

"Aww, I love when you talk social to me."

Geoff grinned and rolled his eyes. "Yes, PR Queen. I know the secret to your heart."

Maybe he did, after all. It felt like he was peeling back all her layers, and she was letting him right in.

"Hey, speaking of which," Avery said. Geoff gave her a look, and she hurried to explain. "I mean about PR! Not about the secret to my heart!"

Oh damn. Always with him. He just laughed and plated a few pancakes on his white dishes, squirting a dollop of whipped cream on top in the shape of a smile. "Go on," he said.

"I know that our collaboration episode worked out pretty well for you." Avery twisted her hands together. "I mean, I looked ridiculous. But whatever. You got good stats off of it, right?"

Geoff nodded.

"Maybe you could bring on X Enterprises as a sponsor down the line. I haven't run it by my team, but if you wanted to send me rates, maybe we could talk about it."

He cleared his throat and rapped his knuckles on the table. "You said yourself that sex toys are the kind of thing that you'd usually introduce later in the game, though, right?"

"When you're dating someone?" Avery frowned. "I guess so."

"So maybe it wouldn't fit the vibe of the show right now."

"Oh, right." She shook her head, her chest tight. Geoff was still going to run a dating show. Things hadn't changed between them. Hell, judging from the lack of angry text messages on her phone, he still hadn't told Sophie about the two of them. And if he couldn't even tell his sister, how was he going tell his audience?

Geoff covered her hand with his, brushed a thumb over the back of her hand. "I'll think about it, okay? I'm still not sure what direction I'm going with things, Cheese. But that's the great thing about being your own boss. You can adapt."

"Adapt. Right." Like Sophie had said.

Geoff snapped a picture of their place settings, the pancakes and orange juice he poured displayed like a welcoming slice of his morning.

Pancakes for two, he wrote in the caption underneath. Then he spun the phone to Avery before he posted the photo online.

"Pancakes for two," she repeated. The thought of it made her chest heat, and she smiled back at him. She didn't need to push things with the show or their relationship—Geoff would come along at his own pace. There was no need to second-guess him.

She returned her gaze to the plate of pancakes. "I've gotta say, that looks really delicious."

He cut a forkful from his stack and held them out for her to eat.

Avery closed her lips around the food, and the sugar spiked through her blood. She and Geoff? They were going to be fine.

"First we eat," he promised, "and then I have a treat for you."

"You do?" she asked.

The gleam in his eyes told her it was going to be good. "I do."

CHAPTER 20

*E*lliot Bay Bookstore smelled like paper and hope. Like ink and coffee. Like hardwood floors and cedar shelves and homemade Nutella pop tarts. Outside the store a steady rain had picked up, the sky zinging and electric and filled with the smell of fresh, earthy soil.

Petrichor.

"What's that?" Avery asked, tilting her head up to Geoff. "Petrichor?" He must have said it out loud.

He squeezed the hand she'd placed in his. "The smell of rain."

"You're such an English major," she teased.

His chest tightened. "Does that mean you don't like the bookstore?"

"Are you kidding me?" Avery's eyes brightened. "I love it. You're forgetting who you're talking to."

He nuzzled the side of her head. "Impossible."

She grinned up at him, tracing her fingers over a hardbound copy of *Practical Magic*.

Geoff nudged her side. "You keep eyeing that one."

Avery blushed. "This is going to sound silly to you, but when I was a little girl, there was a copy of it in my local library that I just loved. I checked it out so many times that the librarian told me I'd reached my limit." He could picture her, a young Avery with big eyes and a wide smile,

129

chewing her lip in concentration as she read. "After that, I wanted my own copy," she continued, "but they'd come out with all the new copies that had the cover from the movie version. And, you know, that's not the same."

"Not at all." He grinned at her. Who knew that a distrust of the movie version of books was a shared connection? He'd always felt that way, too.

Geoff lifted the book from the shelf and clutched it against his chest.

"What are you doing?"

He held Avery's eye. "I mean, right now I'm browsing. But I'm going to buy this for you."

He'd buy her a hundred copies on a hundred different days if he could keep her smiling like he could do no wrong.

He traced his finger down the spine of the book. "Why this story? What about it?"

Avery's eyes took on a sheen of excitement, so bright in the dark day. "I love the idea of magic, that there's something more than you can see in the everyday. I kind of took that idea and ran with it when I went to college, tried to make everything beautiful with my words." She blushed. "Anyway, it's also a story about love—between men and women, sure, but between sisters, too." She flicked her eyes up to his. "Also, there's a rabbit."

"Why do I feel like the rabbit was the real thing that won your heart?"

Avery grinned. "I never had a pet, but I always imagined that if I picked, I'd have a rabbit. And when I grew up, I planned to do magic tricks and grow flowers that made the whole street smell like the sweetest memories you could imagine."

"Wow," he breathed out. "Some book."

She gave him a shy smile. "It is."

"Then I'm glad you get to take it home with you."

She leaned onto her toes and kissed him, and her touch sent all the dark shadows skittering to the corners of the room. "I'm glad I get to take *you* home with me."

"Me too." Geoff backed her against the wall, kissing Avery until her shoulders bumped against a bookshelf filled with fiction, a hundred stories and hundred lives crammed between the pages. She giggled, and his chest loosened. He pushed a lock of hair behind her ears and opened his heart to her.

"I think I'm falling for you, Cheese Girl."

Her grin was electric, cosmic. They were atoms and moon dust and tiny, sparkling particles of stars.

"It's all part of my evil plan," she whispered, and he sealed his mouth over hers.

The kiss deepened quickly, Avery's heart slamming against his. She slipped one hand up the back of his shirt, her palms hot against his skin.

"Bathroom?" he whispered as his cock tightened, and she nodded, tugged his hands.

They stumbled through the aisles, giggling like children, and made it into the tiny room. The bathroom only held a toilet and a sink, but it would do.

Geoff locked the door tight behind them, swung his gaze back to her. "This has gotta be fast, Cheese."

"Not a problem," she said. "I'm already so turned on."

She was wearing a short skirt and tall boots, and Geoff pushed her skirt to her waist, slid her underwear aside so he could feel her. "So wet for me," he groaned as he slipped a finger inside her.

Avery grinned. "Told you so."

He swirled her arousal onto her clit, and she rode his hand, her hips pumping for him even as she unbuttoned his jeans.

All the air escaped from the room, leaving him breathless. "I need to be inside you, Ave." There was nothing in the world more important than this.

Geoff reached for her, so eager, so urgent. The idea of not being inside her right now was unbearable, and he groaned as he shoved his boxers down just far enough to free his cock. He'd always loved sex, but sex with Avery had become a need, a demand. The moments they were locked together in intimacy, nothing else mattered except for her. Here he could keep her heart safe at the same time he shattered her body.

Their teeth knocked together as they fumbled for buttons, pawing through layers of clothing. Geoff rolled on a condom while she braced one hand on his shoulder, the other against the wall. Then he lifted her, the corner at her back taking some of her weight off of him. He pushed her underwear to the side and lowered her down onto his cock, the air hissing out between his teeth at how wet she was. This was so wildly different from anything before, all this connection, like light was going to spark off of them every place they touched.

Avery stood on the tiptoes of one foot as she took him, the other wrapped around him, her heel digging into his ass. Her head tilted back, her body thudding against the wall as he fucked her, raced with her, needing her to take his terrified heart and make it whole.

"So good," she said. "You're making me dizzy."

He smiled against her mouth, then moved his face to growl into her ear. "Turn around."

She dropped her foot and spun, bracing a hand against the wall and dropping the other to circle her clit. Geoff gripped her hip with one hand, cupping the other over her hand on the wall and holding them both upright as he slipped into her again.

"God, I really can't get enough of that," she panted, pulsing back against him, accepting him like he belonged inside her from the start.

"I can't get enough of you."

This time the pace came easier, a tireless rhythm where their bodies took over and they moved like one, the heat and the sweetness building, the explosion inevitable, impending.

Geoff felt Avery's body tighten, stiffen, and he kissed her shoulder as she came. Then his fingers flexed against her skin as he followed her, collapsing against her back, the two of them this laughing, sweating mess.

Maybe this was what people were always smiling about when they talked about being in love.

Maybe this was what it felt like—the whole wide world outside while you locked yourself in a tiny room and saw stars.

CHAPTER 21

"*Y*ou know what I just realized?" Avery asked.

Sophie looked up from the sugar cookies she was frosting and fixed her with a desperate look. "That the wedding of the century is in less than three weeks and I still haven't nailed down the perfect cookie design to wow the masses and skyrocket my business to the top?"

Avery nodded slowly. "That. And also that the wedding of the century is in less than three weeks and I don't have anything to wear."

Sophie snorted and returned her attention to the cookie sitting on her kitchen counter. "I'm not too worried about your ability to pick something gorgeous to wear. You always look put together and beautiful."

Avery frowned and reached for one of the cookies that Sophie had rejected because it was, in Sophie's words, "trying too hard." As if a cookie could try to do anything but taste good. "Maybe we can help each other out," she said. "We nail down this design today, and then we take a break from all the sugar and go shopping."

Sophie raised her chin and smiled. "You're on."

"Good." Avery bit into the cookie, the sweet dough and frosting mixing together on her tongue. "For the record, the taste and texture of these cookies are perfect."

Sophie brightened. "Really?"

"Yes, really. You are a genius, and everyone's going to love you." Avery eyed what was left of the cookie in her hands. It had Vanessa and Jeremy's initials frosted in deep blue over top of the birch tree motif they were repeating throughout the decor. "When it comes to the design, I know you said this was trying to do too much. And I agree that you're cramming a lot onto two square inches of cookie. I think you need to simplify."

Sophie looked at the cooling rack, where the frosting on a dozen cookies was setting to the perfect consistency. "Weren't you the one who told me to keep things on brand?"

"Totally. But you could divide and conquer." Avery popped the rest of the cookie into her mouth and chewed thoughtfully. "Why not do two separate versions where you split out the design elements? One cookie could have their initials, and the other could have the tree motif. You could change up the color of the background and the accents for each design. I bet they'd look pretty striking together."

Sophie grinned. "You are a genius."

Avery gave a small curtsey. "Thank you, thank you. Though, I can't believe we spent so much time on something people are going to devour in ten seconds flat."

Sophie shot her a look. "You should see how much time it takes just to decorate a smoothie bowl to share on Instagram each morning."

"Well, whatever you're doing, it's working for you." Avery brushed the crumbs from her hands. "Anyway, now that we've solved the great Cookie Debacle of the Century, can we please go shopping?" She pressed her hands together and made puppy-dog eyes at Sophie. "Pretty please?"

Sophie set down her icing tips and rubbed her palms over her apron. "Let me frost one sample of each design, and then you're on."

Avery grinned. This was going to be fun.

* * *

"THIS IS AWFUL. Why did I leave dress-shopping until the last minute?" Avery twisted her hands together and stared down at the skirt of the dress she'd slipped on. It was one of those poufy designs that could have been super flattering on the right woman. Instead, she just looked pregnant.

"Let me see it," Sophie called through the fitting room door.

Avery grimaced at herself in the mirror before stepping out to show Sophie.

"Yeah, definitely a no-go," Sophie agreed. She craned her neck to peer over Avery's shoulder into the fitting room. "But what was wrong with the black one?"

"Too predictable." Avery made a face.

Sophie frowned. "You're putting a lot of pressure on a dress."

Avery sighed. "It's just that I want to look perfect." She started rambling, that quick way of talking she had when she got nervous. "It's a big work thing, and it'll also be the first time I'm out as a couple with—"

Holy shit.

She'd almost let the cat out of the bag.

She slapped a hand over her mouth, and since that was also the most obvious thing ever, she tried to pass it off like she was covering a yawn.

"Gosh, anyone else super tired?" she asked. She turned away and pretended to study herself in the mirror. "Must be the sugar crash hitting. I should have cut myself off after three cookies."

Sophie was not buying it. "Excuse me, did you say 'couple?'"

She was definitely fucked.

"Um, maybe?" Avery lifted her eyes and met Sophie's gaze in the mirror. Her friend wore a mischievous expression, her eyes narrowed, but a smile on her face.

"That's what I thought. So, spill. You're seeing someone?"

Avery slipped back into the fitting room and closed the door between them.

"Yeah, I am."

She didn't want to lie to Sophie. Hell, her best friend had been there for her through so much—from her family finally finding its way again after her dad found consistent work, to both of them going off to college. Sophie had listened on the phone for hours after Avery's ex had broken her heart, had sent her just-because flowers and chocolate. Avery and Geoff needed to get their act together and bring Sophie up to speed or shit was going to hit the fan.

She unzipped the hideous dress and pulled it over her head in a cloud of charmeuse and chiffon.

"At least that explains why you've been so mysterious lately." Sophie snorted. "I was starting to think you were ditching me because I always smell like sugar these days."

That made Avery smile. "I'm sorry, but how could that be a bad thing?" She reached for another dress and pulled it over her head. The skirt on the deep-blue dress grazed right above her knees. The dress had a fitted silhouette, and though it had sleeves, they were made of lace, so her skin showed through in a sexy peekaboo effect. The whole thing was fun but sophisticated, and it didn't hurt that it totally fit Vanessa and Jeremy's color scheme.

Sophie's bright voice filtered through the slats of the dressing room door. "Tell me about your mystery man. Would I like him?"

Avery's cheeks heated, and her voice came out small. "Yeah, I think so."

"Great! When can I meet him?"

She bit her lip and forced her voice to stay neutral. "Well, um, he's going to be at the wedding. So, I guess you'd see him there."

Shit. She hadn't even thought about it until now, but that put a very real deadline on spilling the beans to Sophie. Maybe it would ease the knot in her chest that she got every time she lied about herself and Geoff. Or maybe Sophie would disown them both. Hard to say.

"Awesome!"

But it wasn't at all.

Avery stepped out of the dressing room and did a little spin for Sophie. "What do you think?"

"You're gorgeous. Can you dance in it?"

Avery busted out the Macarena, then mimed a conga line. She grinned at Sophie. "I think we've got it covered."

Sophie's clapped her hands together and smiled. "Then you've got yourself a dress, you heartbreaker, you."

CHAPTER 22

"*I* like your costume," the woman in the sexy nurse outfit purred. She skimmed her mouth over the edge of her drink like she was trying to show off the power of her pout, but since she only held a ubiquitous red Solo cup in the hand that wasn't occupied by a stethoscope, the move didn't have quite the intended effect.

Geoff made himself nod, grimacing as her hand landed on his bicep. His eyes swept the room, searching for Avery, searching for Sophie. Searching for any excuse to wriggle free of the eager nurse, really.

The house party Sophie had hooked up for them this Halloween was surprisingly busy, given that it was a weeknight, but it helped that the hosts had done the place up. Fake cobwebs hung from every surface of the Victorian house's lower level, and tall black taper candles flickered on the drink station and buffet tables in the formal dining room. Dim lighting and a low, sensual soundtrack enhanced the mood, and all around the house people clustered together, inhibitions long since gone.

"So, are you a big literature fan?" the nurse asked.

Over her shoulder, Geoff caught sight of Avery entering the room. "What? Um, yeah..."

He let his voice drift off, his throat too thick at the sight of his girl to do anything more than stare.

Sophie's invite to the party had come at the last minute, but somehow Avery had managed to pull together a miracle of an outfit rather than the kind of hack job costume he'd thrown together. She wore an elegant, sexy black gown that dipped low in the back, and her hair was loose around her shoulders—tousled in a way that made him want to run his hands through it and use it to pull her toward him. But the magic of her costume was its simplicity—the only other item she wore was a black mask that looked like it was made of filigree lace. It cast her eyes into the shadows, made her more mysterious and alluring than he'd ever seen her. A striking red lip highlighted a mouth he wanted to devour, and the bodice of her gown pushed up her breasts in a tempting display.

God, she was gorgeous.

And she was his.

"Those books are some of my favorites," the nurse was saying, but all Geoff could notice was the way his heart stopped when Avery caught his eye. Just a whole pause, his blood traveling through his veins—a skipped beat, the rush of wind in his ears.

Avery's eyes dropped to the nurse's hand caught on his arm, and her lips pulled together in a frown.

He should play the part, stay away from Avery and be the dating expert he just told the nurse he was. But all he cared about was that some guy had just approached Avery, handing her a drink. The stranger in a tux was stealing her attention, making her laugh. In their formalwear, they looked like they belonged together, and Geoff bristled.

He moved without thinking, leaving the nurse propped up against the wall with her mouth rounded in an O.

He strode across the room, and Avery's eyes flew open behind her mask as he pushed past the James Bond wannabe.

"Avery," he breathed into her ear. He pressed a hand against the small of her back, which was exposed by the low dip of her dress. Her skin burned hot under his palms, and the smell of strawberries and chocolate filled the air. If he didn't get her out of here soon, he might lose it. "Can I see you in the bedroom? You seem to have a wardrobe malfunction, and it's probably better if we discuss it in private."

Her eyes sparkled, and she let out a low, throaty laugh. "Sounds like a big problem."

"Oh, it is. Huge."

Avery excused herself from James Bond and followed Geoff through the winding house and up the stairs, biting back a smile.

It was reckless, sneaking around together in a house where his damn sister was partying, but he needed Avery. Now.

Geoff pushed open the first door he saw, relieved to find a darkened master bedroom. He locked the door behind them, backed Avery against it and had his mouth on her neck before the latch was even fully in place.

She moaned and raked a hand through his hair, sending lighting tingling down his scalp.

His cock hardened against her hip, and she leaned into his touch.

The words slipped from her lips. "So about that wardrobe malfunction."

He pulled her to him. "I know I complained about your red lips before, but I'm going to take back every bad thing I said about them."

"You like?"

"God, yes, Ave. I fucking love."

Her eyes widened under her mask, and he crushed his lips to hers. He was going to make a mess, but it didn't matter. She was here with him tonight, all layers of silk and satin, and her eyes a beacon in the dark. Her mouth tasted like wine, and he drank her in—the fruity, intoxicating taste of her.

Avery pulled back, breathing heavy, her eyes dark with arousal. "I approve of your approval."

Geoff spun her away from the door, walking her backward until they bumped into the velvet-covered chaise stretching across the foot of the bed. When the edge of the bench hit the back of his knees, he sat down hard and pulled Avery down onto his lap.

He kissed her like the world was ending, stroked a hand up her side and held the other against her bottom, holding her into place so he could buck his hips against her, his cock notched against her slit, separated by layers of clothes.

"Oh my god, Geoff," she moaned.

"Quiet," he whispered. "This needs to be fast."

Geoff helped Avery balance as she climbed to her feet, unbuckled his pants as she slid her panties over her high heels and stepped out of them. She spared a glance down his body and grinned. Geoff wore a tight gray long-sleeved T-shirt with a bunch of gray Home Depot paint swatches pinned to it. "Fifty Shades of Grey, I take it?" she asked.

He nodded back at her. "I thought it screamed, 'I'm literary and also super sexy.'"

She rolled her eyes. "It screams something alright."

He narrowed his eyes at her. "You're going to be screaming something, too, if you roll your eyes at me again."

"I certainly hope so."

Avery grinned and peeled his shirt off his body so the swatches wouldn't cut her delicate skin. Then she lifted the skirt of her dress and climbed onto the bench, a knee on either side of Geoff's body. She braced herself on his shoulders and slid onto his cock, everything wet—hot sensation and lust.

Geoff's eyes shut at the moment of pure pleasure, and he reveled in the bliss of Avery's body squeezing around him. "You're mine," he groaned.

"All yours."

She began to move quickly, taking her own pleasure from him, her motions becoming more and more frantic as she fucked him, her breath shallow and wild. They were getting good at this, learning each other's bodies, something familiar yet new every time. He guided her as she rode his cock, felt his balls tighten at the same time that she began to stiffen.

"I want you to come so hard, sweetheart. I want you unable to walk."

He pushed the top of her dress down and took one creamy breast in his mouth. Avery's head lolled back, giving him access, and he flicked his tongue over her nipple. She spasmed against him, writhed silently, save for her ragged breath.

"Geoff," she whispered, a plea and a salvation wrapped into one cry.

He didn't see her come, but he felt it, her body clamping down around him, milking him, so he exploded, too. "Avery, god—" he called, his orgasm brutal, fast, and hard.

Avery dropped her forehead to his, and they sat silently in some stranger's master bedroom, his heart so loud in his chest he was sure someone would hear it and knock on the door.

"Halloween might be my new favorite holiday," Avery whispered at last.

Geoff kissed her gently. "Mine too."

She groaned and pulled away from him. "We should head back. Someone's bound to miss us."

"The only person I care about is right here in this room."

Avery gave him a look that made him feel a million feet tall and pressed another kiss on his lips. "Come on. Although you might have gotten your wish. I'm not sure I'm able to walk."

"Then I'll hold you up."

She tugged Geoff to his feet and handed him his shirt, and he pulled it over his head while she arranged her dress. Her hair was a mess, and her carefully painted lipstick had smeared at the edges, but she was fucking glorious.

"Was this a trick or a treat?" he asked her.

"Definitely a treat."

"Good girl." He slipped his hand back around one of hers, fully intending to keep his promise of holding her upright as she opened the bedroom door.

Avery pulled open the door and stopped so quickly in the threshold of the doorway that he bumped into her.

"What's wrong?" he asked, and then he looked over her shoulder.

Geoff's chest squeezed, and sharp prickles ran over his skin.

Oh, holy shit.

CHAPTER 23

"*W*hat the hell is going on here?" Sophie stood in the hallway outside the bedroom with a red Solo cup in hand and the blood draining from her face. She looked back and forth between Avery and Geoff. "No fucking way."

Geoff took half a step forward, his hand still in Avery's. "This isn't what it looks like, Soph."

Sophie's eyes narrowed, and her voice came out cold and hard. "No, I'm pretty sure it's exactly what it looks like. You're fucking my best friend."

Avery's stomach dropped, and her throat went dry. This wasn't the kind of thing that was supposed to happen. She and Sophie had always told each other everything. Hell, Sophie had called her in the middle of the night back in college to tell her when she'd traded in her V-card. And now this secret had been building for weeks.

Geoff's fingers tightened around Avery's hand. "I like her, Soph. I'm not going to hurt her."

But even the confidence and care in his warm, low voice couldn't soothe Avery. Not when Sophie looked at them like someone had kicked a puppy in front of her.

Sophie shook her head, her face pinched. "Not on purpose. But it's what you always do." She'd stuck a whole pack of *Hello, my name is* ___ name tags on her shirt, with a different name on every sticker. "Identity Theft," she had said when she first showed up at the party. Only now her costume echoed Avery's own deceit back at her.

Avery licked her lips, but her voice came out scratchy. "We were going to tell you, Soph. Before the wedding."

Sophie wheeled on her. "And you." She jabbed her finger at her. "You're smarter than this."

"I like him, too, Soph."

Sophie squeezed her eyes shut. "No. Something's going to give and then you're going to put me in a shitty situation."

Geoff's voice came out gruff. "I already told you, nothing's going to change your friendship with Avery."

But maybe this already had.

Sophie rubbed the heel of her hand over her chest. "How long has this been going on?"

"Since the show," Avery said.

Sophie's face went even more pale.

"I asked you if you listened..." Geoff started, but Sophie cut him off.

"Don't. Me not listening to your show isn't the reason you've been lying to me."

Geoff stretched to his full height, and all the paint swatches on his shirt rustled together like leaves on a tree. "Like Avery said, we were going to tell you. And the only reason we needed to keep this from you was because we were pretty sure you were going to overreact. The way you're doing now."

Avery winced. He didn't need to provoke her, but he was her brother. Geoff and Sophie had never held back their words or emotions when they needed to.

Sophie's face turned red, and she shook her head. Her voice rose with every word. "I'm going to guess I'm not the only one you hid this from." The Solo cup crumpled in her tightening grip. "So, now you've gotta ask yourselves, why are you still hiding? Who are you hiding from? Or do you just like the feeling of lying?"

"I want this," Avery said. "And I know that's hurting you, Soph, but I'm tired of trying to do the popular thing. I've spent my whole life trying to not to make waves in my personal life. But this is what I really, really want."

Avery's friend just spun on her heel and stalked toward the stairs, taking them two at a time away from her and Geoff.

Avery buried her face in her hands, and Geoff gave her a quick squeeze on the shoulder.

"I'm going after her," he said.

She nodded up at him, her heart racing but her body paralyzed, caught. "Go," she whispered.

The muscles in Geoff's back rippled as he walked away from her. She knew he'd do the best he could to fix this. But Sophie was right to be mad. They'd lied about their relationship, and then lied about their lies. If Geoff picked his sister, she wouldn't blame him. But she hoped to god he was going to come back.

JAMES BOND WAS SAYING something about cell phone networks when Avery felt the heat of Geoff's body at her back. She'd made her way numbly through another glass of wine after he'd left, and his presence near her body made her sag against him in relief. Feeling anything was better than feeling this panic, this tight-chested fear that she was going to push both of them away.

Geoff brushed a hand over her shoulder, and a shiver raced through her. "We should go."

James Bond looked at him sharply. "I think that's up to the lady to decide. She seemed to be having a good time right here."

Actually, Avery would rather wade into a pool of hungry sharks than hear him talk about service coverage for another second. At least that would be over quickly.

"That's okay," she said to Bond, and his face fell. "It was nice to meet you."

Geoff kept his hand at her lower back as they wove through the crowd and out onto the street.

Until the October air swirled around her bare shoulders, Avery didn't realize how hot she'd gotten, how flushed her skin was. Low clouds scuttled across the moon, and the crowds who'd flocked to the streets when they'd arrived at the party had thinned. The only trick-or-treaters on the streets were high schoolers now—ones who'd thrown together makeshift costumes and who carried glow sticks instead of flashlights as they drifted door to door.

"Going to call us a Lyft," Geoff said, and Avery winced.

Sophie had been their driver tonight.

Not anymore.

Avery wrapped her arms around herself as her heat leached out into the cold.

"Is she going to forgive us?" she couldn't help but ask.

Geoff studied her face, his features hard. "Yeah, eventually. You sooner than me, probably. You've got the female advantage. Like some sort of shared brainwaves."

She tried to smile at his attempt to make her feel better, but dread pooled in the pit of her stomach. "Where do we go from here?"

"Right now, we go home."

A Nissan Leaf slid to the curb in front of them on cue, the Lyft driver offering his greetings as they slid into the backseat.

Geoff gave the driver directions to her house, and they rode in silence through the streets of Seattle, the driver fiddling with the radio, *Thriller* playing at a low volume with a watered-down effect.

They pulled to the curb in front of Avery's apartment building, and she climbed out onto the street. She turned when Geoff didn't follow, a light sweat on her skin. "You want to come in?"

He rubbed a hand over his jaw and gave her a pained look, but he shook his head. "I think with the way everything went down tonight, it might be better…"

His voice drifted off, and he sighed.

"Right," she said, too brightly, a band-aid over the cut of his rejection.

"Right." Her heart galloped in her chest, and she wasn't sure she had enough air in her lungs to force more than another syllable from her lips.

Avery closed the door behind her and stood on the curb, watching until the Leaf pulled from the curb and the taillights of the car turned around a corner. Disappeared.

CHAPTER 24

Geoff rolled out of bed on Saturday morning, his head pounding and his mouth dry.

Maybe the vodka tonic before bed last night hadn't been wise. But it had sure as hell been necessary. It had been a few days since the Halloween disaster—one month rolling into the next—and the change of seasons reverberated in his bones. He'd become hollow inside, any new emotion bound to echo.

Geoff had spent the time sending idle texts to Avery, half-hearted attempts to let her know he was there. But he'd milked the few days until the weekend, telling himself he was giving her space to get her work life back in balance.

He was a chickenshit, so there was that, too.

Maybe Sophie had been right after all. Not about hurting Avery, but about how this was going to drive a wedge between the three of them. And despite the fact that his little sister was a giant pain in the ass, it had been a few years since he'd had a huge network in Seattle. He needed every friendly face he could get, and Sophie was one of the good ones here. She kind of had to like him.

Geoff rolled out of bed and padded into the studio, hoping work would help. Even though his programming break had been self-imposed, every episode he didn't record was one fewer opportunity to pull in sponsorship money. And that money was what funded his life.

He clicked open his email and skimmed the latest message from his contact at Slay All Night.

Geoff, it seems like your show is going in a different direction than where our brand is headed, and I don't know if we can keep going along for the ride. This break might be a good time to reevaluate our relationship. If you can share some of your plans for the episodes in the upcoming season, it might help us understand if our relationship can continue to be a fit or if we'll need to part ways. Please send us the latest.

What? *No.*

Geoff's hand twitched around the computer mouse, the bite of the plastic in his palm grounding him to the here and now. Those fuckers. His show subscriptions were up, and episode downloads had reached an all-time high. How did three little episodes about Avery change things?

Geoff pushed back from his chair and paced through his apartment. First the fight with Sophie, now the message from Slay All Night.

He was good at reading signs, and this was a fucking billboard.

Something needed to change.

He reached for his cell and pulled up Avery's number. Typed out a text message, tightened his fingers around the phone. *Can you come over?*

Hit Send.

AVERY APPEARED in Geoff's doorway like a mirage, even though the display on his phone showed that he had, in fact, summoned her. She wore a crimson boatneck sweater, her face pale above the fuzzy neckline.

"Hey," she said, and he stepped back to let her in.

How did he do this? He had to keep himself from reaching for her—it was only going to hurt more if he did—but his fingers twitched with the effort.

Geoff led her into the living room and nodded toward the couch. "Why don't you have a seat?"

Avery's face tightened, and she wrapped an arm around herself like she could feel the air changing for the worse. "I'm good. What's up?"

He closed his eyes. Opened them to find her staring at him, her face already falling. He steadied himself with a deep breath, but the whole world spun. "I've been thinking a lot about what happened the other day with Sophie."

She nodded but didn't speak.

"And I'm starting to think she might be right."

"You're right." Avery frowned. "We shouldn't have lied to her. It was wrong."

He swallowed hard. "Not about lying, Ave. About us. I don't know if I'm built for relationships, okay?"

Her mouth twitched. "Me neither, but I'm willing to try. What we have is really fucking good, Geoff." She blew out a frustrated breath. "You know, part of this is on me. I was so worried about losing you and how that would look that I didn't tell you what I really want. But if the secret's out, we don't need to keep running away. I want this, okay? I believe in it. Do you?"

Geoff ignored her question. "If I had this kind of fallout when all I did was tell my sister about us, what's going to happen when I tell my fans?"

Avery stiffened. "I'm sure your fans will love and support you."

"Not all of them."

She shot him a look. "Weren't you the one who told me you're not trying to impress everyone? That your hardcore fans are going to love you either way, and that rest of the people didn't matter?"

Well, fuck. She wasn't the only one whose words could come back to bite them in the ass.

"Maybe you're right." A muscle tensed in Geoff's jaw. "But I do need to impress my sponsors above anyone. I got a message today from one of the higher-ups at my top advertiser, Ave. They want more programming like what I delivered in the past, or they're going to pull their funding."

Avery's voice came out flat. "And what you gave them was a single guy playing the field." Geoff couldn't look her in the eye, but it didn't stop him from catching the way she shook her head. "So you're going to listen to a stranger instead of me?"

"Not a stranger. I've had a business relationship with them for the past three years."

Avery's voice shook. "And that counts more than whatever you and I have, right?"

He felt so fucking helpless, defending himself when everything she was saying was true. Because yeah, his job mattered to him. It was the thing he'd built, the thing he'd been able to cling to no matter what other shit life had thrown at him. On his show he was important—not the abandoned kid whose dad had bailed on him after the divorce. He was the star.

"I don't know what you want me to say, Avery."

"I want you to say that you'll figure out another way to deliver programming in a way that lets you be happy, too."

"I need to impress these guys."

Exasperation pinched her voice. "They're just one company! You're buying into this idea of scarcity, but there are always more opportunities if you look for them."

He had to hope there'd be other opportunities with girls too since right now he was walking away from the one relationship that had felt so critical to him.

"You know you just spent all this time talking about other people," Avery said, her voice shaking, "but you still didn't answer my question. Do you want this?"

Geoff lowered his eyes to the floor and shook his head. This relationship hurt too much to be the right thing for him. "I don't know what I want. But I know what people expect of me."

"Geoff, people expect that one of these days the dating expert will find the right girl and know when to stop looking." Avery pressed her hand to her chest. "And me? I expected you to know the difference. You might not know what you want with your career and your life, and that's okay. But if we're going to have a relationship, the only right answer is me." She dropped her hands from her body. "At least, that's the answer I know I deserve."

Avery clenched her jaw and strode past him. Out of his apartment and out of his life, and he watched her go without speaking.

She'd never sat down at all.

CHAPTER 25

"*Y*ou look like your cat just shit the bed."

Avery glanced up as Naomi dropped into the desk chair next to her, and Avery's face crumpled. "What do you mean? I look awesome."

She'd pulled together a power outfit to trudge through this Monday at work—a form-fitting dress, killer red heels, and a face full of makeup that hid the bags under her eyes—hoping that looking the part would lift her spirits. It's what she'd always done. Even back when her family was poor and she had to wear the same outfit two days in the week, she'd do her makeup differently just to make it look like she was wearing something brand new.

But according to Naomi, there was no hiding the heartache on her face.

"Your outfit is fantastic." Naomi frowned. "But your face looks like something stinks." She used the pen she'd carried over to nudge the Tupperware container that held Avery's lunch. "Or maybe that's just your salad. I thought you'd moved on to more delicious options."

"Yeah, well the more delicious options are bad for me."

Naomi shot her a look. "Why do I feel like you're talking about more than just food?"

"Because I am."

All Geoff did was prove that theory.

Avery sighed and dropped her fork into the container, then pushed the whole thing to the edge of her desk. "What's going on?"

Naomi consulted the notebook she'd carried with her. "Vanessa asked me to stop by and see if she could snag ten minutes of your time. She's on a call right now, but if you head over to her desk in five, I bet she'll be ready for you."

"Thanks, Naomi." Avery stood and smoothed her hands over her skirt. "I'd better pull myself together. Don't want to look like the cat shit my bed."

Naomi winced. "Sorry, that might have been a little harsh."

Avery waved away the apology. "It was a big shit."

Naomi snorted out a laugh. "If it helps, I think you're awesome."

"It does." Avery gave her a watery smile.

She ducked into the bathroom to gather herself together, then headed toward Vanessa's desk. Even though Vanessa now ran the X Enterprises charity contributions committee and was marrying the owner of the company, she'd kept her original desk in the middle of the Sales area. As Avery strode toward it, a view of downtown Seattle filled her view. The days were shorter now, but at least up here they could take advantage of what little light they got.

The tall buildings of the skyline were pitched against pale gray clouds, and seagulls wheeled on gusts of wind. If only Avery could feel that carefree herself.

Instead, she was a lead balloon dropped off the fifty-sixth floor.

Vanessa turned as Avery approached her desk, her face lighting. "Hey, Avery."

"Hey. You rang? Or rather, you sent Naomi?"

Vanessa nodded. "I wanted to check in on Operation Cookie. I'm going to reach out to Sophie later today, but I wanted to know if you've gotten any sneak peeks of the goods."

"Yep." Avery's stomach sank. On top of losing Geoff, she didn't have Sophie, either. And apparently, the world was going to keep throwing that back in her face. She'd picked him and lost both of them. Some game.

Avery had tried to reach out to Sophie after Halloween, but all her apology texts went unanswered, and there were only so many times she could send a crying cat face emoji without a reply.

She forced a smile now. "I did see the cookies, and they look great. Taste fantastic, too. Your guests are going to love them."

Vanessa clapped her hands together. "I'm so happy to hear that! My maid of honor, Bea, was a little surprised when I told her I was giving Sophie the job."

"Oh. Really?"

Vanessa laughed. "Yeah, Bea used to work at an erotic bakery, and she thought she'd get tapped to make the cookies." She shrugged. "These days she's painting full-time, and I figured it would be a safer bet to use Sophie. No penis cookies necessary."

Avery couldn't help but smile. "Probably not wedding-appropriate. But for the bachelorette party…"

Vanessa blushed, her blue eyes sparkling. "Someone else is planning that, so there's no saying what might happen. I can't be held responsible."

"Sounds like fun."

Vanessa lifted her eyebrows. "Guess we'll see. By the way, I'm excited to meet your date for the wedding. If he's the same guy who sent you the flowers, you're a lucky girl."

Yep. The world was definitely rubbing it in.

Avery made her voice go bright, but all she sounded like was a half-manic Valley Girl. "Totally."

It was too soon for the truth. Too soon to admit that she'd lost out to Geoff's career. She couldn't handle it, and no one needed to see her cry.

CHAPTER 26

*G*eoff stepped through the doors of Portage Bay cafe in Ballard on a Friday morning two weeks after his breakup with Avery. The smell of French toast, bacon, and strongly-brewed coffee wafted over him, and he had to give himself a pat on the back for creating a job that let him work whenever he wanted so he could avoid Portage Bay's normal weekend crowds.

Sophie stood by the wall of flyers just inside the restaurant's front door, clutching a ceramic cup of complimentary coffee.

She sighed in his direction but otherwise ignored him. Apparently, the silent treatment was in full force.

Geoff read the flyers over his sister's shoulder—the MoPOP had a new exhibit, *The Twilight Zone* was being performed live onstage next week, and there was a Thanksgiving Day Turkey trot coming up. At last, the hostess took mercy on them and seated them in a sunny spot in the front window.

Sophie plopped into her chair across from Geoff, waiting until they'd placed their orders before she finally spoke. "For the record, the only reason I'm even meeting up with you is for Mom. We need to figure out what we're doing for Thanksgiving and since you, prodigal son, have returned to Seattle to grace us with your presence, you can actually help plan a thing."

"Okay." Geoff spread his hands. "I'm here because I'm on board. You can email me whatever details you want, and we'll make it the best Thanksgiving ever."

Sophie gave a noncommittal shrug and took another sip of her coffee.

Geoff groaned. "I get that you're still mad at me. But you don't need to worry, okay? Avery and I aren't together anymore."

Sophie's shocked expression transformed into anger, and she leaned over the table to punch him on the shoulder. "Why the hell did you do that?"

"What the fuck, Sophie?"

The mom at the table behind Sophie glared at him, putting her hands earmuff-style over the toddler smearing strawberries onto the fabric napkins.

Geoff rubbed his shoulder. He shouldn't have taught his sister to throw a punch so well. It hurt more than he'd expected. "I like how you assume this is my fault."

"Isn't it?"

Well, shit. "I thought that's what you wanted," he said instead of answering directly. "For me not to date her."

"No! You don't understand people at all." Sophie frowned at him. "I want you to be happy, you moron. And Avery, too."

Their waitress delivered two plates of breakfast to the table, and after Sophie topped her pancakes with fresh fruit and whipped cream from Portage Bay's signature fruit station, she returned to the table to continue her rant. "You know," she said, pointing a fork at Geoff, "I think you and Avery might have been happy, too. Until you fucked it up."

The lump of French toast he'd swallowed stuck in his throat. "Guess it doesn't matter either way."

She huffed a sigh. "You are supremely stupid."

"Hey."

She gestured at him. "I mean right now. Not in general. In fact, your show had some good dating tidbits." Her mouth quirked into a smile. "I liked your whole three-act structure."

He blinked at her in surprise. "You listened?"

"I might have caught a few episodes after Halloween." Sophie dropped her eyes. "We weren't talking. How else was I going to hear your voice?"

It made Geoff feel loved, despite everything, and he held out another tidbit like the peace offering it was. "Want to know what stupid piece of my own advice I took?"

Sophie took a bite of her food and shrugged. "Do I?"

"I broke up with Avery at my house."

Her confused face said more than enough. "Why?"

He sighed. "It's supposed to be easier on the other person. The theory is if you break up with someone in a place that the other person goes every day or sees a bunch, it sucks for them because they keep seeing the breakup place and it hurts them that much more. If you do it at your house, the other person won't tie bad memories to any place except your house."

"O-kay," she drawled.

"Except now I can't stomach the sight of my own apartment." He'd spent the past few weeks crashing at Ryan's house and playing an unhealthy amount of *Grand Theft Auto*, all to avoid the sight of his own bed.

"Ah." Sophie nodded. "Tough break. Maybe you need to replace those bad memories with some better ones."

"Yeah." If only it were that easy. Everything about his place reminded him of Avery—even his damned recording studio, which was the cause of this whole mess. Or, at least, part of it.

Sophie slid her last bite of pancake through a pool of maple syrup. She shoved the food into her mouth and then stood and grabbed her purse. "I'll send you over some Thanksgiving ideas after I get done dropping off wedding cookies tomorrow." She waved at her empty plate. "You're buying breakfast, okay?"

Geoff rubbed a hand over his chest. "Kick a man while he's down." He wasn't sure what hurt worse—forking over the cash for his sister's expensive meal or the reminder of the wedding he'd bailed out of.

Actually, that was a lie.

The wedding hurt worse.

A lot worse.

Sophie rolled her eyes at whatever face he was making. "Whatever. Since I'm feeling generous, I'll give you some advice for all your troubles."

Geoff smoothed a hand over his jaw. "What's that?"

"Go listen to your shows, too, okay? They're not so terrible. You might find what you're looking for." She pressed a kiss to his cheek and left.

THE GREAT THING about *How to Hook a Hottie* and the age of the internet was that Geoff could listen to his show from any place he could get a cell phone signal. After he paid the check in Portage Bay cafe, he wandered out onto the sidewalk in Ballard and plugged his headphones into his phone. Then he opened his podcast list, selected an episode at random, and hit Play.

He listened to his show as he strolled down the street toward the Ballard Locks. The Locks were a series of canals that connected Lake Washington with the Lake Union, and they were always a popular tourist attraction. The water levels in the two lakes were uneven, so the locks served as a passage point between the bodies of water where all the boats could get either lifted or lowered to the right level.

He hunched his shoulders against the damp, chilly morning, and it took until he'd passed through the botanical gardens and emerged onto the docks before he got over the strangeness of hearing his own voice.

A few recreational boats had lined up in the smaller lock, and as Geoff stepped onto the swinging walkway overlooking the lock, the sight of two kayaks down in the water made his chest squeeze.

That day on the water with Avery had been a gift. And he'd traded it in for the stability of a few extra advertising dollars.

He was such a shit.

Geoff turned his attention back to the show, where he was talking about moving back to Seattle and how he was looking forward to reconnecting with the friends he'd left behind. How he'd missed the authenticity of sitting down with someone who really seemed to care, rather than bounce off of the New York bubble everyone seemed to construct around themselves.

He remembered recording the episode, sitting in his New York apartment with the smell of Chinese food drifting up from the street below. New York had been nice, but it was expensive, and the whole time he lived there he'd kind of drifted. Playing the dating scene was fun, but eventually everyone was so tied up in their work that they forgot how to connect.

On the show, he told an anecdote about how his mom had refused to buy Sophie a cell phone until she'd turned sixteen and needed one when she drove, and how his sister's friends just showed up at their house, unannounced. How an open-door policy in a physical way reminded you to keep an open-door policy in your heart. That love and other possibilities could show up any time. Even though Ryan had shown up on Geoff's doorstep more often than not, nothing made Geoff's pulse race like when he pulled open the door and saw Avery.

He clicked on another show and heard himself talk about a girl he knew growing up who could make you smile just walking into the room. He'd told all his listeners to keep an eye out for that feeling, the feeling of a person who could turn your whole world upside-down just by sitting there, watching TV.

And another episode, more recent, from after his first date with Avery. He described the feeling of kissing her, and how you had to seize the moments when they finally came.

On and on Geoff clicked, skipping segments, listening to random bits while he watched the locks fill with water. He listened as the water lifted, as the kayakers made their way through.

Oh shit.

He'd recorded three seasons of episodes as a single man, but it was no wonder he'd never gotten serious with anyone. The whole time he'd been saving this spot in his heart for Avery. Even when he didn't say her name, even when he hadn't known it was her, she'd been there.

He loved her.

Geoff could hear it in his own voice, and he'd just done the stupidest thing he could, pushing her away.

After everything, he'd told Avery this breakup was about the show, but she'd been part of his success all along.

Geoff stepped over the bridge from one side of the locks to the other, the water rushing underfoot like blood in his veins. He had to make things right, but he didn't know what he could do to fix the mess he'd created. Or if there was even time.

CHAPTER 27

*a*very stepped out of her cab and tugged down the hem of her dark blue dress. She was glad for the way the sleeves protected her arms against the chill, but any comfort she had dissolved as camera flashes exploded around her.

Dammit.

She'd drafted the press release for today's wedding and run it by Jeremy and Vanessa yesterday before they left the office. When they'd given her the thumb's up and thanked her for her hard work, she'd sent it to a few of the top news outlets under strictest confidence. But somehow the paparazzi had still appeared, DSLR cameras in hand.

Avery gritted her teeth as she stepped inside the Arctic Club Hotel, glad she wasn't famous. Also glad she'd managed to hide her puffy eyes under a layer of makeup.

"Avery Beeker, get your gorgeous butt over here!" demanded Emma Harrington from outside the doors to the Dome Room, the Arctic's signature ballroom.

Avery hugged her clutch to her stomach as she threaded through the crowd toward the blond Quality Manager, smiling as Emma pulled her into a hug. Bex Kingsley, X Enterprises' lead product designer, followed suit, then both of the Las-Vegas-based women introduced their dates.

Fiancés, actually.

Because a wedding was a perfect place for more soon-to-be-married couples to show off their love, along with their gorgeous engagement rings.

Not that Avery was bitter or anything.

"Alone today?" Bex asked, looking over Avery's shoulder.

"Afraid so." Avery's stomach flopped, and she squeezed back a pang of regret. Dammit, she'd wanted Geoff here—to dance with her, to laugh with her. But mostly just to be with her. Too bad wanting didn't change things.

Emma tsked. "Maybe Jeremy has a hot single friend for you." She lifted an eyebrow and grinned. "You never know."

Avery's smile was so forced it made her head hurt. She didn't want any random hot single guys. She wanted Geoffrey. For all the good that did.

"It's okay," Avery said. "Anyway, my friend's doing the favors, so I'm not totally alone."

Except Sophie still hadn't spoken to her, so it was mostly a lie.

"Let's go find our seats," Avery suggested, hoping to take some pressure off this rapidly dying conversation.

Bex's fiancé, Gabe, held open the door to the ballroom and waved her ahead. Avery stepped inside the venue and gasped.

"Breathtaking, isn't it?" Bex asked from beside her.

"Literally."

It's no wonder the Dome Room was famous. The enormous space featured a huge stained-glass dome, with Rocco gilding and ornamental cornices lofted over a wedding aisle decorated with candles and a white silk runner. Original frescoes embellished the walls of the venue, and the air smelled like the soft white flowers that covered every surface.

Bex gestured at the seating area, a sea of chairs with ribbons laced through the spokes of the backrests and plush white cushions covering the seats. "Bride's side or groom's?"

"Both?"

They laughed and took their seats spread across the aisle, Bex and Gabe on one side, Emma and Deacon and Avery on the other. Sean, one of the

Sales team members, took the empty seat next to Avery, and she let him pull her into idle conversation as the room filled with guests.

The noise level in the space rose as people greeted each other and showed off their wedding finery, but the scale of the huge room still dampened the noise. For all the grandeur of the room, the wedding wasn't huge. A manageable number of people filled the room to create the perfect blend of intimacy and glamour.

At the front of the room, a violinist played a small, sweet song, and the room hushed with expectation. Avery turned her eyes toward the back of the room, where Jeremy's groomsmen had started to proceed down the aisle.

Ramon Rodriguez, X Enterprises' Sales Manager and Jeremy's best friend, led the procession, his handsome Hispanic features pulled into a proud smile. Jeremy followed close behind with what must have been a custom tux clinging to his body. When you looked at him, it was easy to forget he was standing here, getting married. Jeremy wasn't totally Avery's type, but her boss was undeniably hot. No wonder Vanessa had fallen for him, rules be damned. But if even they could make their relationship work with all the pressure of Jeremy running a company, why couldn't Avery and Geoffrey get past his show?

A dark-haired little girl, barely past the walking stage, toddled down the aisle, a silk basket with white rose petals clutched in her chubby fists. The room gasped and giggled as she started walking, realized everyone was staring, and buried her face in her hands.

You can't see them, they can't see you.

Avery smiled, her chest warming as Ramon stepped forward from his spot at the altar. He kneeled on the ground and opened his arms for his daughter. Emilia wasn't just Ramon's daughter, she was also Jeremy's goddaughter, and the crowd clapped as she scrambled down the aisle and into her dad's arms. A tall woman with gorgeous red curls followed Emilia down the aisle. That must be Bea.

Then the crowd hushed again. Avery ran her fingers over the fine raised ink of the wedding program and returned her eyes to the back of the room. A bridal processional began to play, and the doors swept open once more. Avery and the other wedding guests rose to their feet as the doors revealed Vanessa's silhouette, elegant and beautiful in a mermaid-cut dress.

Avery wished she didn't feel so alone in the room as Jeremy met his bride at the altar, wiping away tears. She wished Geoff was here to hear the couple repeat their vows to each other, to promise to love each other even when things got rough. She didn't need to marry Geoff. She just needed him to try.

That was the sticker out of all of it. Geoff had been part of her life for so long that with him it had felt like they were skipping straight to the good parts. Only now they'd skipped straight over any of the happiness into this disappointment that crushed her chest like someone had driven a tractor-trailer onto it and parked. This bitterness that tasted like ash in her mouth.

Avery smiled and clapped for the couple as Jeremy dipped Vanessa in a back-bending first kiss. In a few more hours Avery could go home and climb into her bed and pull the covers over her head for the rest of the weekend. But for now, she needed to be strong. This was just another mask to wear. It was a matter of survival, of getting through.

"You ready to go?" Sean asked, turning to her.

She realized she'd been standing there, staring at the now-empty altar, for long enough for the whole wedding party to have walked back through the doors.

"Home?" she murmured.

Sean pointed to the adjacent room. "To cocktail hour and then the reception. There's still a party to enjoy."

Of course there was.

Avery took the arm Sean offered her. "What are the odds of an open bar?" she asked.

Sean met her with a smile. "Very good odds. Outstandingly high."

CHAPTER 28

*G*eoff stabbed the End button on his cell phone to drop the call, then tossed it on his couch. It wasn't as effective as slamming down a receiver on a landline, but he'd have to work with what the technology gave him.

"How hard can it be to get a tux in this town?" His jaw was wired tight enough that he could pass as a Nutcracker ornament at Christmas, and even his teeth hurt as he ground out the words.

Ryan pointed at Geoff's discarded phone. "Harder than you thought."

Geoff grunted. *Thanks, Ryan.*

"Yeah. Harder than I thought." He rubbed a hand over his face.

"Why can't you just go to this wedding in a nice suit?" Ryan asked.

"I need to make the best possible impression. I need to show Avery I'm serious about our future. Make a grand gesture. A suit says, 'I showed up in what I had lying around.'"

"But it's true."

Geoff shook his head. "Don't care. I need a tux. Do you know anyone who might have one? Friends, parents, siblings…"

Ryan scratched his knee. "I mean, my brother did jazz band thing back in college, and if I remember correctly, he might have had to buy a nice outfit."

"A tux?"

Ryan shrugged. "Something fancy."

"Okay, I'll take it. Get him on the phone and tell him we're on the way."

Ryan shook his head and reached for his phone while Geoff raced into his bedroom and pulled a backup suit from his closet. Ryan was hanging up as Geoff returned, and Geoff looked at him expectantly.

"So?"

Ryan nodded. "He does, indeed, have a magical tux."

"Magical?"

"Apparently it's the key to getting laid." Ryan grinned.

"Let's hope so."

Ryan inspected Geoff's body and frowned. "I don't know that it's going to fit you."

"It'll have to work."

Geoff combed through his pants and pulled out his car keys, then pushed Ryan out the apartment door.

As they stepped onto the elevator to ride down to the parking lot, Ryan raised an eyebrow. "What time does this thing even start?"

"Um, six?" Geoff guessed.

"You don't know?"

"I never officially got an invitation. Everything went to Avery." The elevator doors opened with a ding.

"Does that mean you don't know where we're going either?"

Geoff gave him a look and stepped through his apartment building's lobby and into the parking lot outside. "Minor details."

Ryan threw his arms in the air. "Not minor details. Major details. The most important details of all."

Geoff pressed his car keys into Ryan's hands. "That's why I need you to drive. I have some calls to make."

Geoff hung his suit on the hook in the backseat of the car, then pulled out his phone and dialed as Ryan drove in what was presumably the direction of his brother's house.

"Sophie, hi," Geoff said when his sister picked up the phone. "I need your help."

"Hmm," she said. "That's not the best lead-in to a conversation I've heard."

He gritted his teeth. "Look, I'm sorry for everything that went down with me and Avery."

"Are you?" she asked without heat.

"Of course I am. And like I said the other day, I'm sorry for the way I lied to you. I'll say it until the day I die if you help me."

Sophie sighed. "What do you need?"

"Avery booked you that wedding job for her boss, right?" Avery had done too good a job keeping the press for this wedding under wraps, and the internet search Geoff had conducted earlier hadn't returned a venue for the wedding. There wasn't going to be a grand gesture if he couldn't find the damn location.

"She might have."

"Jesus Christ, Sophie." Did his sister have to be a pain in the ass today?

"Okay, yes. She did get me the job. Why?"

"Where's the wedding being held?"

Sophie probably didn't mean her laugh to sound so mocking, but it did. "That's confidential information. Jeremy and Vanessa literally had me sign an NDA."

"I'll give you twenty bucks."

Sophie scoffed. "You've never bribed someone before, have you?"

"A hundred bucks."

"A hundred bucks and an explanation," Sophie said. Geoff could picture her smile.

"It's for Avery." His heart raced even saying her name. "She's the one, Sophie."

"Oh god, are you going to make me throw up in my mouth?"

"I'm going to throw up if I don't get there in time."

Sophie's sigh was a happy one, and he knew he had won. "Are you going to remember the name of the hotel, or do I need to text you?" she asked.

"I'll remember," Geoff promised. He would commit the information to heart.

* * *

RYAN EASED Geoff's car into the valet station in front of the Arctic Club Hotel and cut the engine.

"You sure I can't crash this wedding with you? The more the merrier."

Geoff opened his mouth. "This is something I need to do—"

"I was kidding." Ryan smiled. "I'll leave your car with the valet and catch a Lyft home. Maybe even grab a drink at the bar first."

Geoff tightened his fingers on the door handle. "Thank you."

"You're welcome. And for what it's worth, you look good." Ryan's brother had come through, and the tux he'd bought for his jazz band escapades fit Geoff almost perfectly.

Geoff nodded his thanks and opened the door.

"Go get the girl," Ryan called, and Geoff strode through the hotel doors and into the lobby.

A concierge stood behind an elegant desk, shuffling papers. "Can you point me toward the Glass and Reese wedding?" Geoff asked the man. "It's being held here tonight."

The concierge eyed him up and down. "A little late, no?"

"Am I?"

"The ceremony started at five. I'm afraid you might have missed it, sir."

No. He couldn't have. Geoff glanced at his watch. Seven-thirty. "But the reception?" For all the money they were shelling out for this place, it had to be here, right?

The concierge tipped his head. "The Main Dome Room." He pointed in the general direction. "But you'd better hurry."

Geoff didn't just hurry.

He ran.

He arrived at the Dome Room breathless. Dance music filtered through the thick doors, and his heart leaped at the thought that they hadn't left yet.

They had to still be here.

He swung open the doors, staggered by the massive size of the room. How was he going to find Avery in this giant space?

The room had a romantic vibe, complete with candlelight glittering on every table. Silver highlights accented the room's cream and blue decor, and some of the tables held low, elegant flower arrangements, while others held centerpieces made of tall, scraping flowers. Half of the wedding guests sat at the tables to enjoy dessert, and the other half twirled on the dance floor. A scan of the room told Geoff it would be hard to find Avery without going spot to spot. Unless...

He approached the DJ, a guy in his mid-thirties standing behind a complicated projection booth.

"Can I put in a song request?"

The guy nodded at him, and Geoff shouted the song name over the noise of the song. The strains of *Sweet Caroline* faded out, and the unmistakably iconic beat of *Wannabe* by the Spice Girls rose up to fill the silence.

Mel B sang about what it took to be her lover, about forgetting the past to embrace the future, and a wave of goosebumps raced over Geoff's skin.

He skimmed the room, looking for movement. For Avery.

There.

Toward the back of the room he caught a flash of brown hair, the gorgeous curves he'd come to love. He knew the shape of her in a crowded room, had memorized the freckle on the left side her neck, knew the way her body would move as she danced.

And he'd known she would dance for this song.

Avery hadn't spotted him yet, but Geoff glided across the floor to her, savoring this moment of anticipation. She wore a long-sleeved blue dress with a lacy bodice that gave him a hint of her creamy skin underneath. She was so familiar that his knees went weak at the sight of her, and his stomach twisted in a knot that only her smile could soothe.

She drew him in without knowing, and he came to her. They were magnets, after all. Once they connected again, he was going to make sure they were inseparable, but right now they hovered somewhere between push and pull.

Elbows and knees struck out as people danced to the upbeat song, and Geoff dodged them, making progress across the room until a woman with

sky-scraping heels stepped directly on his toe. Geoff winced but perse-
vered. "Avery," he called, and his girl spun.

Her eyes widened, and she froze, her mouth dropping open.

"Geoff? What are you doing here?"

He gathered his courage and opened his mouth to win her.

eoff took a step forward, and Avery's chest tightened.

"What are you doing here?" she asked, swallowing a rush of tears. She refused to let herself react to him, but he was here, wearing a tux unbuttoned just enough to show off the kissable skin of his neck, his warm eyes filled with hope and longing. Lights from the DJ's setup scattered over his skin and highlighted the angles and planes of his face, and he looked so damn good.

Avery's heart lodged in her throat, and the whole room swirled—not just because of the lights on the dance floor.

"I'm here for you, Ave. I don't want to run away anymore."

Her heart pounded so hard she could feel it in her fingers, and her throat went dry. "Is this why Sophie cornered me in the restroom and told me not to leave until the end of the wedding?"

Sophie had given her a funny look over the plush hand towels at the bathroom sink, or at least it had seemed that way at the time. Avery had since had at least two more glasses of wine, so the details were a little fuzzy.

Geoff's lips quirked. "It might be." He leaned closer to her ear. "Can we go somewhere to talk?"

Sean, who'd been dancing a few people away, noticed the way Avery had frozen on the floor, and he spoke up now. "Is that okay with you, Ave?"

She could see the way Geoff bristled and drew himself up to his full height, and she nodded. "I'm fine."

She motioned toward the far side of the room, and Geoff closed the distance between them, placing a hand on the small of her back to protect her as they wove through the crowd. His touch burned, and her body begged to lean into it, but she pushed back her shoulders and made her spine go straight and tall.

They emerged from the group and moved toward the wall, and somehow the air felt clearer already, just by being off the sweaty dance floor. Avery moved away from Geoff's touch and leaned her shoulders against the wall for support.

Geoff turned to her, his eyes sweeping over her body with a mixture of appreciation and concern. "You're gorgeous," he whispered.

"I am…" she faltered. "Drunk. Open bar." Dammit. Avery shook her head. It was so hot in here. "I mean, thank you."

Geoff cracked a smile. "You're welcome, Cheese Girl. You always did have a way with words."

She narrowed her eyes at him. "Why are you here?" She leaned forward an inch, equal parts nervous and eager for what he had to say. Over Geoff's shoulder, the party was continuing on, but here in this bubble it was just his body and hers and the way she tried to stop herself from jumping into his arms just because he'd shown up.

Geoff took a deep breath "I know I told you that weddings represented the death of a single man."

"I do recall," Avery said wryly. The memory of that revelation still stung.

"Well, I don't want to be a single man anymore, Ave."

She searched his eyes, and all she saw was how heartsick he looked. Was that the same expression on her own face right now? It was the way her chest felt, anyway, trying to expand under the weight of the pain that had crushed it these last few weeks.

Geoff continued, his voice low and thick. "You were right, you know. I spent all this time shutting myself off and not fully committing to anyone, but I think it's because I got caught up in this girl ten years ago and never really got over it."

"Oh." Avery's heart dropped, and she lowered her gaze.

Geoff brought a hand to her chin and lifted it, so she was looking him right in the eye. "It was you, Ave. And once I had you for real..." His throat bobbed as he swallowed hard. "I didn't know how to stop being the single guy. But god help me, I want to try."

Her chin trembled as she spoke. "You do?"

"I'm here, Ave. I want to be your lover. I want a future with you, and I know I haven't been perfect in the past. But I want to try. So, so much."

Avery twisted her hands together. "Did you just quote the Spice Girls at me?"

Geoff cracked a smile. "I might have paraphrased a bit." His smile grew. "You like my song choice?"

"I love it." She gathered her courage because it was now or never. Show her cards or let this crash and burn. If Geoff was trying, she was going to try, too. "And I love you, you know."

Geoff nodded, his face so full of relief and joy. "I do know that. And I love you, too."

"Really?"

He ran a hand over her jaw, and she leaned her cheek into his palm. "I've loved you for years, Avery Beeker. It took me a while to stop trying to be who everyone else wanted me to be. And right now, I just want to be who you want me to be."

"All I want you to be is you." A thought made her pause. "But what does this mean for the show?"

"It's going to have to grow with me, Ave. My audience deserves to know that all the methods I teach aren't just for a night. That you can find someone to build a whole life with."

Geoff leaned forward, then, and brushed a tentative kiss on her lips. Avery's whole body sang, and she rose onto her toes to kiss him back. As the kiss deepened, she drew her arms around his neck and held him tight, his heart against hers, the world on fire.

Geoff finally released her, and she dropped onto her heels to look up at him. "Where do we go from here?" she asked.

"Home, Ave." He smiled at her, all hers. "There's something I need you to hear."

CHAPTER 30

"*W*hat I need to hear is in your studio?"

Avery paused at the threshold of the door, an uncertain look playing across her beautiful features.

Geoff nodded and pulled her against his side. He'd driven them back to his place, one hand on the wheel and the other hand in hers the whole ride over, the quiet car full of all the unspoken things they hadn't said. Now that she was here, that she'd agreed to be his, that she'd said *I love you*, he craved the contact of her skin on his.

He pressed a kiss against her hair. "Trust me, okay?"

She nodded. "I do."

Geoff led Avery into the studio and sat on one of the desk chairs. Then he pulled her onto his lap, arranging her legs across his and looping one of her arms around his neck. She nestled her head under his chin as he leaned forward and started up an episode of *How to Hook a Hottie*.

Geoff watched her face change, moving from confusion to disbelief to acceptance as she listened to him talk, telling his audience about her, sometimes subtly, sometimes not.

He went back in time, further and further, into New York and beyond, and let her hear his heart on the line.

"Even when you weren't in my life, you were in my life," he whispered. "More than you or I ever knew." His arms tightened around her. "Letting you go was the biggest mistake of my life."

Avery nodded. "It's only a mistake if you don't learn from it." She smiled and poked a finger into his chest. "And if you do it again."

Relief washed over him. "Not going to happen, Cheese Girl. I'm in it for the long run."

"You are?"

He nodded. "I also had one more thing I wanted to run by you. I mentioned that I want the show to go in a new direction, and while I'd love to still help out single guys, I also want to talk about how to keep a relationship healthy, sexy, and fun long past those first three dates."

She smiled at him. "I'd listen to that show."

"Good." He grinned back. "And you know what's better than one person talking into the ether?"

She cocked her head at him, a glint in her eye. "Two people talking into the ether?"

"Exactly. Any chance you'd consider hosting the show with me? Just an hour-long show one day a week, and I'd do all the social media and run the business side."

"An hour a week?" Avery pulled on a frown. "I don't know if that's going to work for me."

"Oh." Geoff shook his head. *Right.* "Too much going on in your other job?"

She shook her head, a teasing look in her eye. "I mean I might need at least two hours." She brought her lips to his ear, a gust of warm air making him shiver. "I have a lot to say about keeping your love life sexy."

Geoff brushed a kiss against her neck. "I hear you're the industry expert."

Avery laughed. "I might need to work on my on-the-fly speaking skills. But practice makes perfect."

"Right. And speaking of which, we should probably go practice some of those techniques for keeping the flames hot."

"Should we now?"

Geoff nodded. "We should."

Avery giggled as he lifted her and carried her to his bedroom. She moaned into his mouth as he kissed her and laid her on the bed. She let him love her the way he'd wanted to ever since he'd walked away from her, mouth and hands and skin and heart, and she breathed for him, moved for him, rose up to meet him at every turn.

Geoff had spent the last three years mixing sounds on his show—adjusting volumes, erasing background noise, balancing tones. But Avery's voice as she called his name was a light in the darkness. It might be the sweetest sound he'd ever heard.

* * *

A KNOCK on the doorframe of Geoff's bedroom woke him, and he shifted, Avery's soft cheek still pressed against his bare chest.

"Is everybody decent in there? You better be, 'cause I'm coming in."

He barely had time to nudge Avery awake and pull the covers over their naked bodies before Sophie burst through the doors, a Tupperware container clutched in her hands.

His sister took one look at them, covered her eyes, and screamed. "I asked if you were decent!"

"You didn't give us time to answer."

"Get dressed, and then we need to talk." Sophie turned her back, giving him time to pull on a T-shirt and toss a second one to Avery.

"We're decent," Avery called with a smile. "More than decent, actually. We're glorious."

Sophie turned and rolled her eyes.

"What are you even doing here?" Geoff asked.

Sophie pouted. "I was hoping you'd have made up with each other so I could make up with both of you. I even brought apology muffins."

"Sounds good to me." Avery made grabby hands at Sophie, who cracked open the Tupperware and tossed a muffin at her. Avery peeled back the wrapper and took a huge bite. She smiled at Geoff around a mouthful of blueberries and cornmeal, her eyes bright. "You know, maybe this could be our first segment for the show. What to do when you fall for your best friend's sibling."

He shot a glance at Sophie. "Or, more like, how to not kill your sister when she cock-blocks you."

"Eww!" Sophie screeched, throwing a chunk of muffin at his face. "Don't ever say the words cock-block to me again."

"Sophie! You're going to get crumbs in my bed."

"Pshht, Avery started it. Anyway, I'm sure there's already far worse in there." Sophie screwed up her face. "Oh god. I can't believe I said that." She groaned and pointed at him. "You're paying for the cost of my therapy."

"I don't know if I make enough money for that."

His sister shook her head and gestured around his room. "Have you seen your fancy apartment? Somehow I doubt that's true."

Avery giggled, and Sophie cracked a grin. "Are we good again?" Sophie asked quietly, looking at the woman by Geoff's side.

Avery blew out a breath. "As long as you know that I'm not planning to choose sides between you two. And that I love you both."

Sophie's eyes widened. "You love him?"

Avery's shy smile made Geoff's heart just about leap out of his chest. "I do."

He pulled her close to him, muffin crumbs at all. "Say that again, Cheese Girl."

"I love you, Rock."

He cradled the back of her head and brushed his lips over hers. She tasted like blueberries and hope, like a future where they took today and kept on climbing. "I love you, too."

In the background, his sister sighed. "Guess you're both re-invited to Thanksgiving."

"I'll bring a side dish," Avery offered.

"See?" Sophie said to him. "You could learn a thing or two from your girlfriend about being helpful."

His girlfriend. It had a really nice ring to it.

"Any idea what you want to make?" Sophie asked.

Avery grinned at both of them, a sparkle in her eye. "How do you feel about macaroni and cheese?"

Geoff smiled back at her. "Personally, I'm a fan."

EPILOGUE

"*L*adies and gentlemen, you heard it here first. The latest X Enterprises Lovers' Kit is the perfect way to get the sparks flying in your love life, whether you're rekindling an old flame or starting something new." Geoff shot the computer camera a cheesy grin that showed off his gorgeous mouth and made his eyes sparkle. "Totally not influenced by the fact that my girlfriend works for the company."

Avery laughed and rolled her eyes, knowing the audience watching the live-stream and listening to the podcast loved their banter. "Not at all."

They'd announced the new direction of the show right after Thanksgiving, and Avery had helped Geoff rebrand *How to Hook a Hottie* into *How to Keep a Hottie.* She'd even designed a new logo and everything, and whatever she'd done—no, whatever they'd done *together*—had worked. *How to Keep a Hottie* had received more downloads than *Hook to Hook a Hottie* ever had, and widening the scope of the show had allowed Geoff to bring on a bigger variety of sponsors. Including X Enterprises, who'd reported their own increase in revenue tied to the ads.

That's what you call a win-win.

Avery shifted in her chair, leaning closer to Geoff so the heat from his body warmed her side. On the computer screen, the two of them looked so happy together, and his voice in her ears was a lifeline, a love line, the answer to everything she'd wanted. She looked into the camera and smiled. "But all that aside, there's no time like the New Year to try new things and take your relationship to the next level."

"Is that so?" Geoff asked.

"Totally."

His grin widened. "How about for me and you?"

Avery couldn't hide her blush, and now the damn cameras were going to make sure it lived in infamy on the internet, too. She bit back a grin and met his banter. "If you're talking about doing something wild in the bedroom, we might want to take that conversation offline."

"That's not exactly what I had in mind, although I wouldn't complain." Geoff's face softened and grew more serious, and he reached into the pocket of his pants. "I was thinking of something more like this."

He lifted a jewelry box and opened it, a thin platinum band set with diamonds sparkling against the black velvet cushion.

Avery's heart lodged in her throat, prickles running over her skin. "Wait. What?"

"Marry me, Avery Beeker. You are my past, my present, and my future, and no matter what comes, our love will be perfect because it's ours. We've already started our three-act story. Now let's give ourselves the happy ending that we deserve."

He was serious.

Avery shrieked, a thousand butterflies fluttering in her stomach and her chest, lifting her out of this room.

Geoff smiled, his eyes glassy and his voice thick. "Folks, I'm pretty sure that noise you heard there was a yes. But with all the crying it's hard to be sure."

"Yes!" she shouted, her voice clear and true. She wiped back her tears as Geoff slid the ring onto her finger. She kissed him, not caring about the cameras, the podcast, the world. It was just her and Geoff, together in this room, with the rest of their lives a promise they'd keep on making to each other.

She smiled into his eyes, her hand on his heart. "Now that's what you call leveling up."

THE END

BOOKS BY TANYA GALLAGHER

A Slippery Slope

His Distraction (X Enterprises Book One)

His Inspiration (X Enterprises Book Two)

His Invitation (X Enterprises Book Three)

His Temptation (X Enterprises Book Four)

YOUR OPINION MATTERS

I can't believe we've made it to book four of the X Enterprises series! I've loved every minute of writing this series, especially writing Avery and Geoff's story. If you loved reading it, I'd be honored if you'd consider leaving a review wherever you purchased this book. Reviews help more readers find my books so the fun can continue!

I also love to hear from my readers and think you are just the best. If you join my mailing list, you'll get sneak peeks at future books and be the first to know about new releases.

Join the fun at tanyagallagherbooks.com!

ACKNOWLEDGMENTS

This year I set out to write a few love stories, and somehow that turned into five books and five happy endings, with more stories to come. I wouldn't have gotten here without the amazing people who have helped me on this journey. Seriously, the friendships and joy that have come out of this process are the best rewards.

To my readers - Thanks for being here with me! I loved writing this story, and I'm so happy I get to share it with such beautiful humans. Thanks for reading.

To Jenny - Thanks for all the positive encouragement about this little cupcake of a book. You make this writing journey so much fun, and I'm so glad we get to do this together. You're simply the best.

To my RWA friends - It's so much fun to be part of a community of people who love the same things you do. Thank you for your excitement and encouragement, your words of wisdom, and your friendship.

To Ian and Lily - Thanks for supporting me as I worked on this project, but mostly thanks for all your love. I couldn't do this without you.

To my ARC team - You are incredible! Thanks for taking the time to review and share His Temptation, and for supporting this series. I love that this community has brought us together!

ABOUT THE AUTHOR

Tanya Gallagher is the Seattle-based author of contemporary New Adult and Adult romances about smart, strong women and the sexy men who love them. She traded pencil skirts in the boardroom for stories in the bedroom and hasn't looked back since. You can find her traveling the world in search of beautiful scenery and delicious cake, and at penchantforpleasure.com, where she happens to sell one of the most popular brands of personal lubricant for your naughty bits. True story.

Let's Hang Out

Website: www.tanyagallagherbooks.com
Instagram: tanyagallagherbooks
Twitter: TGallagherBooks
Facebook: tanyagallagherbooks